I0586004

WHERE THE WEIRD

THINGS ARE

Edited by Austin P. Sheehan and Clare Rhoden

First published by Deadset Press in 2022.

© Deadset Press 2022

All rights reserved.

Cover design Copyright © Austin P. Sheehan.

Edited by Austin P. Sheehan and Clare E. Rhoden.

Acknowledgement of Country:

In the spirit of reconciliation, Deadset Press acknowledges the Traditional Custodians of country throughout Australia and their connections to land, sea and community. We pay our respect to their Elders past and present and extend that respect to all Aboriginal and Torres Strait Islander peoples today.

Acknowledgements:

This anthology was put together by a wonderful team of passionate writers, editors and readers that are spread all over Australia. Thank you to Clare Rhoden, Helena McAuley, Maddie Jensen, Mikhaeyla Kopievsky and S. M. Isaac. Thanks also go out to all the contributing authors, and to all those in the Australian Speculative Fiction community who submitted a story. The biggest thanks, however, must go to you, the reader. It is those who are willing to read, learn and share which allow myths and legends to live.

— Austin P. Sheehan, on behalf of Deadset Press.

CONTENTS:

There have been many eerie night-time sightings both above and below the water of Port Melbourne, Victoria.

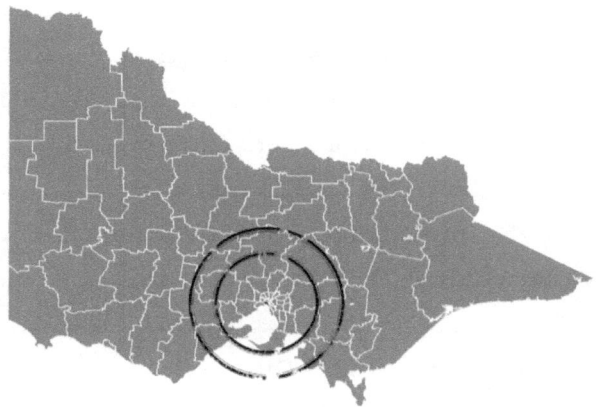

THE IRON SHIP

E. H. Alger

<u>July 1947, Rotten Row, Fishermans Bend, Melbourne.</u>
The sky is low and sullen, the wind incessant. Sliding between
factories and cargo cranes, a slow brown river churns as it
meets the incoming tide. It laps and sucks at the rotten piles of
a wharf where a few coal hulks, hulls red with rust and masts
cut down to stumps, tug like tethered beasts at their moorings.
Perched on a mossy hawser, a night heron stares into the
murky water, feathers gleaming in the dusky light. The sky
leaks darkness; shadows creep and pool.

The shadows gather deep about the largest of the hulks,
moored downstream. Once a big square-rigger—iron hulled,
strong built and elegant of line—decay now drapes her like a
shroud. Her sides are rust-blistered and crusted with coal
grime; slimy weed grows thick along her waterline and trails in
the current like green hair.

Seeping through the dying city noises—a truck grinding its
gears, a horse and cart clattering over cobblestones, the chug of
a steam locomotive shunting wagons in the distant rail yards—

comes a faint sound. It is surely just the wind soughing through rigging, whining and moaning amongst the wires.

But no . . . it sobs like a woman weeping . . . or perhaps she is laughing. Bitter laughter, rasping like rusty iron on iron.

The night heron takes to the air with a thud of wings and flaps away upstream.

An old sailor, trudging cityward, glances up at the beat of wings, trips on a bluestone kerb and curses. He'd been thinking of the sea, deep and dark, of mastheads sweeping a high blue sky, of trade winds, sunlight, and flying fish.

"But I hate the fucking sea." Muttering under his breath, he pulls his coat tighter against the knifing wind. "And I hate Melbourne. May as well live in the fucking Antarctic."

At some point in every voyage he had ever made, over a lifetime of voyages, he'd sworn that as soon as his feet touched solid earth, he'd run inland and never look back. And he'd sometimes done it—bought train tickets for towns as far from the sea as his money would take him, found work cutting down trees or digging ditches, but before he knew it, he'd be on a train again, heading to the nearest port.

Yesterday he'd shuffled up and down gangplanks in Victoria Dock. Today he'd done the same along Southbank. But there's no work for a worn-out old coot when scores of young war heroes are keen for the few jobs going. Seems experience and knowhow mean bugger-all these days.

The sky is leaden, the air smells of coal dust and imminent rain. It's an ugly part of town, south of the river, a scramble of factories and warehouses, concrete and corrugated iron, rust and rot. Newspapers and last year's leaves scurry along bluestone gutters, driven by the interminable wind.

Out of breath, the sailor halts on a corner. He gulps in a wheezing lungful before doubling over to cough. Straightening up, he expectorates into the gutter and gropes in his seabag for his cigarettes, menthol as the doctor ordered. He takes a soothing drag, rubbing at the coal grit in his eyes and peers, blinking tears, at the river. A rusty tug labours past, trailing fumes and oil slick. Upstream the grey stucco walls and orange tiles of the Mission to Seafarers building are visible now between the warehouses on the riverbend. He's almost there. Just a last trudge upriver, skirting the dry dock, to cross the Spencer Street bridge, backtrack downstream and there'll be a firelit room, a comfortable chair, a hot cuppa and a biscuit, and a sympathetic smile from Deirdre, or Doris, or Dot, or any of the other ladies of the Harbour Lights Guild.

He's just stubbed out his cigarette and got his weary legs moving again when someone passes from behind, knocking him sideways. The fellow doesn't turn, but keeps striding along the street, a canvas seabag slung over one shoulder. The old seaman draws breath. He can't see the fellow's ugly mug, but he knows him. The tattoo of a bloodshot eye on the back of

3

his shaved head is a dead giveaway. He knows that pit-bull noggin, hard as a cannon ball, the wiry frame, the bow-legged swagger. Most of all he knows those fists. The man punches like he's swinging ingots of lead.

"Jack fuckin' Driscoll," curses the sailor. "Bastard's going to the bloody Mission." He looks towards the city, then back down the river, unsure where to go. He could jump on a tram back to last night's cheap lodging house in St Kilda, but there were fleas in the greasy carpet and noisy drunks coming in at all hours of the night. One had thrown up in the old man's shoes.

The first drops of rain sting his face and he pulls his coat collar up around his ears. Not too far downriver a coal hulk is moored on her own, one of the few still in use to service a dwindling number of steamships. Smoke rises from her galley chimney and the sailor fancies he can smell something cooking. The rain falls harder as he heads towards her gangplank. He's surprised to see a tricycle and several battered bicycles leaning against the ship's deckhouse, surprised too to see a woman taking washing off a line strung between the mainmast and the afterdeck. She glances at him as she hurries inside with her basket and a moment later a wiry little man comes out to block the top of the gangplank.

"You after somethin', mate?" he asks, holding a newspaper over his head to keep the rain off.

4

"Just a place to lay me head tonight, that's all; the deck'll do as long as it's out o' the rain."

"Sorry mate, not here. Got six kids aboard—two of 'em down with the measles."

The sailor casts an eye over the ship. Though she's battered, rusty and coal-grimed, it's clear she was once a pretty vessel. *"Rona,"* he says. "I crewed in this old girl years ago, just across the Tasman a few times. Nice ship—friendly, honest."

"Still a good ship," says the wiry man, taking one hand from the newspaper to pat the vessel's bulwarks. "Not for long though. No work. Only steamer in port now is the dredge and once that's pensioned off this old girl'll be towed out and scuttled in the ships' graveyard."

"End of an era. Bloody waste." The rain trickles down the back of the old man's collar as he doubles over to cough. "They'll be scuttling me out there soon enough," he wheezes. "Need a fag." He gropes around for his cigarettes.

"Here." The wiry man comes halfway down the gangplank, holding out a light. "Look, if ya head downriver . . . ya know Rotten Row down on Fishermans Bend? Bit of a hike, but there's a few hulks moored there ya can bunk down in. It'll be dry and there'll be coal for a fire." He sidles back up the gangplank, frowning over his shoulder at the old man who hunches over, sodden and dripping, trying to keep his cigarette dry. "Wait here, mate; won't be a sec'."

5

A minute later he's back with an oil lamp, a can of baked beans and a slab of fresh-baked bread wrapped in wax paper. "Present from the missus," he says. "If ya could bring the lamp back tomorrow . . ."

It's almost dark as the old sailor sets off downriver. To the west a dirty orange streak lingers along the horizon, silhouetting a row of factory chimneys that spew smoke into the inky sky. A ship churns its way upriver, portholes gleaming like yellow eyes. The wash from its passing sloshes and sighs against the wooden piles of the wharves. Along the deserted streets lamplight glitters on rain-wet paving.

He's staggering by the time he gets to Fishermans Bend. His knee joints grind, bone on bone, with every painful step. But here at last are the hulks—four in a row, shackled like defeated leviathans to a couple of neglected jetties, their bows towards the land and sterns to the pull of the flowing tide.

The closest he recognises. The *Shandon* had been a fine ship in her day, but now—like all of them—she's a truncated, coal-grimed ruin. Lamplight leaks out from her big deckhouse where, engulfed in a fug of cigarette smoke, several men sit round a table playing cards. The old man feels an odd yearning to join them, but even as he watches, their voices rise in drunken anger. He hitches his seabag from one shoulder to the other and shuffles on past into the darkness.

6

He stops when he sees her, a black shape looming against the black sky. She's moored facing the sea and her imminent grave, and so deep in shadow that he can't even see her gangplank.

Beneath the sheltering eaves of a locked-up warehouse, the old man manages to get his oil lamp lit. Rain flecks the air with gold as he holds the lamp aloft, and the vessel's elegant counter-stern takes shape. Old paint and rust have long obscured her name, but he can just make out the first four raised letters: RANN . . . and, underneath, the name of her homeport: GLASGOW. He whistles softly. "Eh, you were a beauty once," he breathes. "Still a queen under all that rust."

Something niggles at his memory, touches him like a cold hand. He shakes his head, scattering rainwater, and stumbles forward. The barbed-wire barricade rigged across the gangplank does not stop him. He clambers 'round it, cutting his hand and ripping the hem of his coat, then stands on the deck sucking the blood from his thumb and listening to the deep silence.

Such silence: it soaks up distant city noises like a sponge. He closes his eyes, ignoring the rainwater trickling down his collar; feels safe. The old hulk may be a wreck, but she's still a ship and he understands ships, more intimately than all the streets and buildings and crowds and filth and bewildering bureaucracy of the land.

7

He climbs the stairs to the afterdeck. The timbers underfoot are rotting, and everything he touches is grimy with coal, but for now he's captain of his own ship. He descends the narrow companionway into the aft accommodation. Tonight, he'll sup in the captain's saloon and sleep in the captain's bed.

It's not bad down below. The lighterman who last lived here had kept the place neat enough. The old man shines the lamp about the saloon, his eyes widening at the opulence of its etched glass skylight, its walnut and teak panelled walls, its cast-iron fireplace inset with glazed porcelain tiles—all shabby now, with coal dust embedded in every grain and groove.

There's a bucket of coals beside the fireplace and even a wad of dry newspaper. He gets a fire going and heats the baked beans in the can; holds the scorched metal between folded newspaper to scoop up the beans with his pocket-knife spoon. The cheap beans and the bread taste like contentment. Rainwater drips through the leaking skylight to trickle down the slope of the floor, collects against the wall and runs through a door into the chartroom. The old man huddles as close as he can to the flames. He's still wearing his coat and it steams in the heat. Feeling sated and happy, he lets his eyelids close.

He wakes with a jolt as his body topples sideways, flings out an arm and pushes himself upright. His heart beats in shock. He looks round in confusion before remembering where he is. Everything is as it was except that the saloon is much colder.

"Fuckin' icebox in here," he mutters, throwing more coal on the fire.

The captain's cabin is on the opposite side of the saloon to the chartroom—he'd checked it out when he first came down here and seen the horsehair mattress still on the bed. It'd be comfortable enough with his canvas seabag as pillow and his coat as a blanket.

The old sailor struggles to his feet. He glances towards the door to the captain's room; sits down again. A dark shape beside the door makes his heart thud. The weak light from lamp and fire barely penetrates the gloom. He narrows his eyes, and the darkness thickens. *It's just me bloody coat,* he thinks; *I must 'ave hung it up there.*

The air is icy and a sharp, alien odour fills the saloon. It brings images—of a bleak place of drifting mists and drowning bogs.

I'm still wearing me bloody coat. Must be the lighterman's coat left behind.

The darkness shifts, and grows far too big to be anyone's coat. It keeps growing, and the peaty smell is swallowed by a tang of salt and iron and tar.

The odours trigger a memory, clear as sunlight. A wharf in Valparaíso, his own ship in for repairs after a storm. Another ship tied alongside her, a handsome full-rigger who'd lost her foretopmast in the same storm, and a stretcher—the body covered—being carried down the gangplank. Later, a seaman in a bar telling him: "Bloody ship's a killer! Kills a man or two every voyage. It was 'er captain this time, and that man loved his ship, more'n his wife and kids." He tipped his beer down his throat and got up to leave. "Cursed, ya know. A death in the shipyard when she was built, and the mourning widow laid a curse on 'er for all eternity."

"Rannoch Moor," quavers the old sailor. "That's your name. From Glasgow."

The darkness surrounds him, strokes his face, whispers inside his head. *"My burning, bone-crushing birth . . ."*

The clangour of a shipyard accident fills the old man's skull, shouts of alarm, the roar of flames, the screams of the injured. He flinches back from the stink of flesh burnt to the bone. "Why pick on me?" His voice is high-pitched and hoarse. "I just needed to get out o' the rain. What the fuck d'ya want?"

"What do you *want?"* The voice is a rasp, iron on iron.

"I want to go. Let me grab my things and I'll be off."

"You will stay."

"Fuck you!" He scrambles to get up, but his limbs feel like water. "Damn! Bloody hell . . . you're the ghost of that widow, the grieving widow that cursed!"

"Ghost?" Her mocking laugh defiles the air. *"No, I* am *the curse. I am the curse of every widow, every mother, every*

10

woman whose husband, whose son, whose lover, went to sea and never returned." Her form takes shape from the shadows like a nightmare.

"I am the curse," she hisses, *"of every fearful sailor clinging to a footrope above pounding seas. I am the terrified curse of the falling, the agonised curse of the crushed, the choking curse of the drowned."*

Her mouth is a gash in iron, rust-red; her eyes are rivets, rimed in salt and oozing. She stinks of bilgewater and blood.

"I am the pitiless cold, the endless hunger, the wound that never heals. I am the gulfing wave, the howling gale, the bloody eye of the cyclone. I am the salt-crusted, rust-blistered, iron-rivetted heart of the ship . . . and I can feel your ravening emptiness."

"I'm not empty, I've just eaten a fuckin' can of beans!" His voice shudders and shakes as he struggles for air.

"You crave more than food. You are empty. You have nothing. You are nothing."

"No, no, no." He closes his eyes, refusing to see her. "It's you that's nothing. You're not real. But I am *something*. I'm a seaman, and I know ships. Whatever you are, you're not a ship . . . You're not the heart of *Rannoch Moor*. Ships are nothing like you."

Eyes clenched shut, he pushes away from her blood-stinking breath and her rasping cackle, finds his back up against

11

the saloon wall. "Shut up, hag," he spits, "just shut it."
Clamping both hands over his ears, he tries to recite a poem he
knows by heart, a device learnt years ago to stave off
desperation. "These . . . these splendid ships, each with her
grace, her . . . her glory . . ." He forgets lines, puts them in the
wrong order, stumbles over words. "I touch my country's
mind, I come to grips with half her purpose, thinking of these
ships . . ." He gulps air, goes on: "That nobleness and
grandeur, all that beauty, born of a manly life and bitter duty
. . . they are grander things than all the art of towns; their tests
are tempests and the sea that drowns . . ." His voice is stronger
now. "They mark our passage as a race of men—Earth will not
see such ships as those again."

Hunched over, ears clamped and eyes shut, he sits for a
long moment. Slowly, he takes his hands from his ears. The
saloon is silent but for a swishing sigh: water slipping and
sliding along the ship's hull. The deck tilts, and the sailor
imagines the warmth of the sun and a clean salt breeze on his
face. *She's gone*, he thinks, *she's gone*.

He opens his eyes. The filthy shadows have fled and
firelight flickers on the walnut walls. The sailor feels its warmth
on his left arm, his cheek. He turns towards it . . . and she is
there, sitting beside him.

He jumps, flinging himself backwards into the wall as she
turns her eyes towards him. But she is transformed.

She is a ship's figurehead, carved by a master of the art and lifted to perfection by the finest painter. Alabaster skin, rosebud lips, cheeks blushing. There is a glint of gilt on her white, wave-kissed gown and one pale, long-fingered hand clutches a posy of moorland heather to her breast.

"See what you have done," she sighs; *"I have remembered how to be a ship again."* She smiles and the old sailor stares, his heart beating hard again, but for a different reason. His mouth gapes as she tosses the heather aside and rises. She is too tall for the saloon, and she shines like an angel.

"Let us go sailing, my captain," she says, taking his hands and lifting him to his feet; *"just you and me. We shall slip down the sullied river, cross the wide bay and fly from the fetters of land."* She smells of sunshine and her voice is a zephyr. *"We'll snare the quartering winds and cross the seas and oceans of the world. Come! We must catch the tide! Go now, cast off the mooring lines!"*

"Yes, yes," he gasps, entranced, before old habit takes over; "Aye aye, cast off the mooring lines!" Dragging his eyes from her, he makes for the companionway.

Up the stairs to the deck he goes without a backwards glance. He's failed to notice that her skin is beginning to craze. The cankered paint cracks and flakes away, the decaying timber beneath bulging through the gaps like black fungus. The

13

sailor doesn't smell the rot and putrefaction, doesn't hear the rasping laughter begin anew.

Like a man half his age, he runs along the deck to each of the bitts, slackening the springs, the breast lines, the bow and stern lines. A small voice in his head remonstrates with him: *What the fuck are you doing? Are you mad? You're not going anywhere with cut-down masts and no sails . . . one man can't sail a ship this size anyway . . . and there's no bloody food or water aboard.* But he ignores it, for it's surely lying.

He bounds down the gangplank, swings himself round the barbed wire, and dashes forrard to cast the eyes off the bollards. The mooring lines are weighty, as thick as his forearm, but he knows what he's doing; he's done this hundreds of times. *But never on your own,* argues the small voice, *and always under orders.*

He's released all the lines but the aft spring when the ship, nudged by the current, pivots her bow—out into the river. Her stern swings into the wharf, and the spring snaps taut, tripping him up and throwing him off his feet. He falls, flailing, into the narrowing gap between the ship and the wharf, grabs at the bollard, and for one hideous moment feels the weight of the ship crushing the life out of him. But somehow he hauls himself up again. The line released, he chases the gangplank as it drags across the wharf timbers, leaps for it and is back on

14

deck as it falls away into the river. The ship is free and moving fast, her bow towards the sea.

He stands at her helm, the varnished wood smooth beneath his calloused hands. She answers him, so quickly, so kindly. A steady wind sings high in her rigging, her great sails belly and crack as she heels to the breeze and bounds down the bay. The sun rises on her port side, sending shafts of gold into the towering clouds. Gleaming dolphins leap beneath her bowsprit and wide-winged seabirds wheel above her mastheads. The old man looks aft, where the foam-white wake curls behind the ship across an infinity of ocean and knows he need never again touch land. She is all he needs now. She is everything.

* * *

Two days later, the morning newspaper, *The Argus*, prints a quarter column article on page five. The heading reads: "Killer ship claims last victim."

"The body of able-seaman, Mr William Laney, 67, was discovered on Tuesday morning. He had fallen from a wharf at Fishermans Bend on the Yarra River, and been crushed between the wharf timbers and the iron hull of the coal hulk, *Rannoch Moor*. It appeared that he had been attempting to cast the hulk adrift. Mr Laney was not married and has no surviving family. His friend, Mr Jack Driscoll, boatswain, described him as 'a skilled rigger, a loner and a dreamer, and a man who lived for ships and the sea'.

"In a sinister twist to Mr Laney's tragic story, it is known that the *Rannoch Moor*, originally a full-rigged ship built in Glasgow in 1883 for the South American nitrate trade, had an unfortunate reputation as a 'crew-killer'. During her twenty-two years at sea, at least nineteen of her crew are known to have drowned or died accidentally, including one of her captains. In recent years, since her conversion to a coal hulk, lightermen living and working aboard have described the vessel as 'haunted'. The *Rannoch Moor* is scheduled to be scuttled this Friday in the ships' graveyard between Point Lonsdale and Barwon Heads. It might be wise for the tugboat crews, and all of the men working to achieve the sinking, to 'proceed with great caution'!"

November 2020, Ships' Graveyard, four nautical miles east of Torquay.

A small wooden boat bounces at anchor atop the outgoing tide. Inside the tiny wheelhouse a man in a captain's hat fiddles with the radio, while on deck two divers, empty tanks discarded and wetsuits running with saltwater, stare over the side into the darkening waves.

"He's gonna be out of oxygen," says one of the divers, glancing at her watch.

"I told him there'd be too much gunk from the Barwon today," says the other, his voice shaking. "Followed him to that wreck but lost him. It's like bloody soup down there; couldn't see my own hand."

"You got through to Search and Rescue yet?" The woman turns frantically towards the wheelhouse, but the only reply she gets is a string of expletives and the sound of something being thumped. "Fuck," she says. She reaches for her phone again, but it's just as much out of range as it was the last time she checked.

"What about flares? Could we send up an emergency flare?"

The two divers look towards the man in the hat, but he shakes his head ashamedly. "Forgot to bring 'em," he mutters.

They fall silent, the woman scanning the darkening horizon for other vessels. But there's nothing—just the heavy twilight, the slap of waves against the hull, and their own distressed breathing.

"Shit! Did you hear that?"

"Hear what?"

"Laughter! I heard laughter!"

"Out here? You're nuts. Just a seagull squawking."

But then they all hear it. They stare at each other through the gathering darkness, eyes wide, hearts thumping.

"Fuck," she squeaks. "Get the anchor up. We gotta go."

The sun finds a gap in the clouds and shoots a blood-red ray of light across the sea. When it sinks moments later it sucks down with it every last scrap of luminescence.

They'd flooded the engine and flattened the battery trying to get the boat underway, and now they huddle together, shaking with cold, as their vessel drifts alone upon the deep. The sky is starless and moonless, the wind has died. Night presses in, as black and silent as a tomb.

Mute with dread the three stare, wide-eyed, blind, into the void. They make no sound but for their shuddering breaths, their drumming hearts.

Then they hear it again, a laugh that scrapes through the dark like iron on rusty iron.

About the Author:

E.H. Alger grew up in the suburbs of Melbourne. After graduating in art and design she became a freelance book illustrator, working for many of the major publishing houses. She also wrote and illustrated an acclaimed children's picture book, 'Bertie at the Horse Show', published by Penguin.

Her 2018 fantasy, 'Winterhued', was her first novel and she is presently working on a fantasy trilogy.

She's travelled widely, voyaging the world's oceans aboard eight sailing ships, and for many years was a volunteer aboard Melbourne's tall ship, 'Polly Woodside' (formerly the coal barge, 'Rona', that makes an appearance in her story).

She now lives far from the sea in rural Victoria, near the border of Bunurong-Gunaikurnai country, surrounded with rescued animals including several horses and a pet Brahman bull.

Victoria's Otway Ranges can be as treacherous as they are beautiful, containing both wonders and impenetrable mysteries.

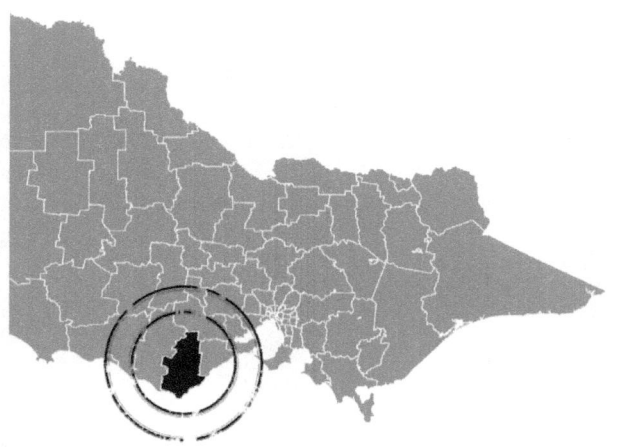

A BEECHY BOY

Clare Rhoden

Jack runs ahead, as he always does. How anyone can keep a close eye on an eight-year-old is a mystery Ellie would like to solve, but this morning is not the time or the place. She increases her pace up the steep, narrow path that leads to the top of the paddock, ears straining to hear how far ahead Jack has run.

"Wait for me!" she calls. "Wait at the gate!" Her words dissolve in the thick mist, cloaking her in a cloudy quilt, as if she never said them at all. The fog is good at blanketing noise, making the world invisible. It smells good, fresh and earthy, like a rain forest should.

Ellie keeps the torch focused on her feet, wary of the gnarled roots that embroider the cleared ground, nearby trees reaching out to reclaim what was theirs. And cow pats, though they haven't seen any cows in the few days they've been here. The website showed quite lovely photos of huge black-and-white heads lined up at the cottage fence, but Ellie is happy to do without that aspect of country life.

"Jack!" she calls again. A muffled laugh from somewhere ahead. She hopes he's not going to play that drop-bear game again, where he jumps down on her from up a tree. She's on her guard, torch tight in both hands, ready to shine it at him.

Ellie reaches the skewed wooden gate that separates this paddock from the Beechy Line. No sign of Jack, but she's come so far up the hill, the fog is lighter. He can't be too far ahead. He wanted to show her things up here, things that look best at dawn or dusk.

She clambers through the uneven bars to stand on the gravel pathway. At this early hour there are no cyclists, and it's unlikely any walkers would have come this far along the track from Gellibrand yet. Ellie looks back down the steep slope to the holiday cottage she chose because Jack was so excited about the remnants of the old Beechy Line railway nearby.

Something swipes past her head, startling her even though it has to be her son playing pranks. A flash of wings and a flurry of air tell her she's wrong, and the next moment she's jumping again as a kookaburra cracks out a cascade of mocking laughs overhead. Jesus. No wonder the first Europeans thought madmen were attacking them.

"Jack!" she calls again, a bit annoyed, though the behaviour of the wildlife is not his fault. The sky is much lighter and she switches off the torch, frowning down at the uneven track.

Uphill to the old bridge, he told her last night, so she starts off in that direction.

"Hurry up Mum! Don't be such a slowcoach."

Ellie's heart pounds once, then settles. There he is, up ahead at the next curve, his rosy cheeks almost as red as his parka. "I can see you, cheeky boy. How far to the bridge?"

"Long way," he calls over his shoulder, and disappears around the bend. "George is gonna meet us there."

George is a local kid, the one who's been telling Jack all about the wonders of the old rail trail, promising wombats and echidnas if they get up here early enough—even a platypus in Charley's Creek, if they're lucky. Ellie hasn't met George or his parents, but Jack told her that George likes to play with the children of families staying at the cottage. He often hangs around waiting for visitors, says Jack, who's taken a big shine to him. This last few days, *George* and *George-says* feature in all his stories.

The fog—or maybe low clouds, she supposes, as the track is so high up the mountain—drifts in and out like a veil, wafting chills over her every so often. She follows the sound of Jack's running and his occasional cries of 'keep up'. She'd prefer to have him in sight, but he's eight now and wants to run. He's almost too big for a goodnight kiss, which is a thing Ellie finds especially disheartening.

She continues uphill, the curving nature of the track preventing her from seeing far ahead. She takes a moment to marvel at how they built a railway through these hills, the terrain so steep and wet. On her left, cuttings lift high above the track, dripping with dew and the last of yesterday's rain. Huge trees—regrowth from the old timber trade—reach high into the mist: mountain ash, stringybark, beech, wattle, the odd apple tree sprung from a discarded core.

On the low side of the track the ground drops away into abrupt ravines, complete with miniature waterfalls soaking down into the tree ferns. Those ferns are beautiful, their curled new growth exquisite, rising above the bracken and blackberry that border the track.

The forest opens a little to her left. A small clearing—what used to be a clearing—shows the decaying trunk of an enormous tree, a dead giant lying at an angle to the track. A ballast siding, that's what it was—Ellie remembers Jack saying so, information courtesy of George, no doubt. Ellie smiles. What a colossal tree that must have been. No wonder the timber fellers loved this forest.

But it's sad, too. No way any tree will grow to that girth in the future. She shakes her head, stops to listen: boyish laughter ahead. She presses on up the hill, hands now dug deep into the pockets of her jacket. The dawn air is freezing. Her nose is

24

cold and she has to stamp her feet every now and then to feel her toes.

The track bends again, and Ellie sighs. So much for a nice mum-and-son holiday, a handful of days to put locked-down home schooling behind them and get ready for the new year. She's hardly seen Jack. All his energy directs him outside, and he's now—so it seems—too old for his mother to tag-along. Ellie remembers a time when she wished with all her heart that he could amuse himself a bit more, keep out of her way. *Be careful what you wish for,* she thinks.

But this is strange new territory, and while she agrees with building resilience and independence and initiative, something about the still, cold air gives Ellie the shivers. Not just the temperature, but how the sun stalls on the far side of the mountain, as if sunrise will never arrive. Plus the fact she's been walking uphill for the better part of thirty minutes and she's still chilled to the bone.

The Beechy Line is not quite the jolly morning walk she expected.

"Jack!" she calls. "Jack! Where are you?"

The kookaburra cackles directly overhead, and there's an echo of laughter further up the track.

Ellie stops to cup her hands around her mouth. "JACK!"

A squadron of rosellas erupts out of the undergrowth. The ground shakes with the beat of kangaroos, bounding away with a sound like a muffled jackhammer. Straining her ears above the wildlife, Ellie hears Jack's voice.

"Up here, slowcoach, by the bridge—what—" The words fracture into a stifled cry, and Ellie bolts toward the place.

Cold air makes her throat and lungs ache as she pounds up the track, eyes wide with fear. "Jack!" she gasps, but the only answer is a scolding chitter from the scrub wrens and another guffaw from the kookaburra. Around the next bend the track descends, and Ellie gulps in snatch of icy air turning her head this way and that, desperate for a sight of him. "Jack!" she calls, dashing down the incline, slipping on the muddy sections, staggering on the gravel, sobbing with terror. Another curve reveals the worn and warped planks of an old bridge, the bridge Jack told her about.

Here's the bridge, but no Jack. The place looks untouched, like a postcard from a bygone age. There's nobody to be seen. She lets out a despairing cry that echoes back from the sides of the cutting, chill and eerie.

Ellie stops, bends double, tries to drag in a breath past the pathetic, terrified flapping of her heart. The bridge is huge and disintegrating. Ferns and moss drape its broken spans. Saplings push through the large gaps that perforate it. The old bridge stretches imperfectly across a huge ravine where a narrow waterfall dashes down the mountain.

Surely, surely the boys didn't try to cross that rotted thing? Surely?

"Jack!" she calls, and then "George!" The water gurgles and splashes below. The damn kookaburra chuckles in reply. Ellie yells, anger bolstering her fear. "Aaargh! Jack, wait till I find you! Just you wait!"

She steps warily onto the first span, leaning forward to peer between the moss-covered beams. There's no sign of anyone below—no red parka, no boyish limbs. Ellie lifts her head to look at the bush on the other side of the ravine. Nothing.

She turns from the bridge, fists clenched. She fights dread and rage. How could a sunrise walk in the rainforest go so wrong? Damn Jack and his stupid friend. Damn the wombats and the platypus and the scarlet robins. Damn her for listening to his pleading. Damn her for—

Ellie stumbles back, mouth gaping, staring at the biggest kangaroo she's ever seen. It must be over two metres tall, standing on the track and blocking her way forward.

Lurid images of injured runners flood her mind, blaring about roo attacks. The kangaroo's face is impassive, its huge dark eyes fixed on her, muzzle down in disapproval. The hunch of its shoulders, the bulging chest muscles, all make her very aware she's an intruder. This is his rainforest.

Ellie has never been so frightened.

She scrambles to her feet, crouching low as she retreats. The buck kangaroo never takes his gaze from her; he even leans forward as if considering a leap. Ellie puts up both hands in supplication, can't help whispering, "Look, see, I have no weapon, I'm no danger to you. I'm leaving now, but, but, my son! Please, please." She doesn't know what she's asking, except perhaps that the animal will let her past, let her find Jack.

The buck lifts his head and lets out a barking growl, loud enough to cover the gushing waterfall. Ellie takes another step back and the kangaroo barks again. Off to the side, as if in answer to the king roo's command, the mob booms through the forest again, twigs snapping and branches swishing as they go. But—wait—was that the sound of a boy laughing, heading deeper into the bush among the mob? Ellie calls out for Jack, and the kangaroo takes a bound toward her. She covers up, crouching low, and in another moment he's gone clear over her, crashing through the undergrowth in the wake of the mob.

She stays low, arms over her head, dragging in air that tastes of fear and forest. Her face is running with tears. She's sobbing. Fright and anger and frustration choke her voice. "Jack," she whispers. "Oh, Jack!"

* * *

The ambulance crew are kind, kinder even than the searchers who've come from Colac, Apollo Bay and as far as Geelong, arriving in batches throughout the day. It's shock, they tell her, and exposure. That's why she's shaking so hard.

They shepherd her toward the trolley. Just to the hospital in Colac, don't worry. The doctors will check you out, make sure you're okay.

"But Jack!" Ellie cries.

"They'll bring him," says the paramedic, soothing. "You can see him there. He's going to Colac too. It's best you don't look now, really. You can visit the morgue later."

Ellie wails. "No!"

"Sweetheart, he's dead. He's had a nasty fall, and then the mob's gone over him—"

"Leave off!" says someone else.

"Sorry, sorry, sweetheart. Time to go. Come on now."

Ellie goes a few steps, her heart and mind still, vacant, empty. Then a single word: Jack, Jack, Jack . . . Suddenly she stops, pulls against the paramedic's guiding hand.

"What about George? Did they find George?"

Murmuring and whispering, she can't catch the words. Then someone says, "Let's ask Danny, he's a Beechy boy."

There's jostling and more whispers. Ellie gets the idea that they've already dismissed George, that they never even looked. Her heart squeezes with pain.

One of the searchers comes forward, a tall, thin fellow with sandy, receding hair. "Danny," the paramedic asks him, "Any chance there was another boy up here? Ellie says she remembers somebody called George, eight or so. He came to play with the boy, with her son, I mean. Anyone of that name round here?

Danny frowns, his face pale under a galaxy of freckles. He seems embarrassed, but at least he looks her straight in the eye. "Sorry, missus, nobody called George around these parts. There's no kids on the farm up there, the one past the bridge. George was the name—" He stops, looks guiltily at the ambulance crew. "There was a George here once, came picnicking with his family one summer. Got lost in the bush. Years ago, if it ever happened."

"Oh, that George!" says the paramedic with his hand on Ellie's arm. She looks at him in bewilderment. He coughs. "That's just a story, right Danny? What our parents told us to keep us from wandering. Don't be like George the Beechy boy, or you'll get lost and never come home. Something like that."

"No," says Ellie. "He was a real boy, he was. I heard him. I heard . . ."

She hears nothing else above the roar of her blood, pumping knowledge to her reluctant brain, her devastated heart.

Her Jack. He's now a Beechy boy.

About the Author:

Clare Rhoden lives on Bunurong country in suburban Melbourne. Author, editor and reviewer, Clare started writing early and never stopped, although she is often interrupted. Her novels are published by Odyssey Books, and her short stories and non-fiction pieces have appeared in Australian and international journals. Her Doctor is Tom Baker and her star sign is Cancer. Come meet her at clarerhoden.com

The spectacular views from Mount Buffalo make it easy to overlook the dangers of the unforgiving wilderness.

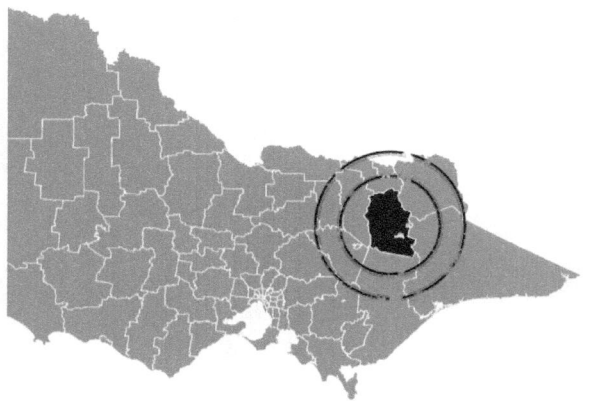

THE CARETAKER

Austin P. Sheehan

It was the perfect job for someone in my position, and more appealing than the alternative. In truth, working on the chalet between the seasons would be somewhat akin to being in the hole. *Nowhere is a person more themselves than when they're alone.* Folk in the villages and towns throughout this sun-blasted colony disguise themselves in an attempt to fit in, trying to keep up appearances, until one day they forget who they really are. Then they carry on, maintaining their airs, with their very identity consigned to oblivion.

"Look after her, and I'll be back to re-open for winter," said the owner, holding out the heavy iron keys.

"Will do. I'm looking forward to spending some time in the country." *And facing my demons.*

"I must say, we wouldn't usually hire a young man from town such as yourself, but your letter of recommendation made a strong case."

I nodded, taking the proffered keys. *My father must be as keen for me to redeem myself and prove myself a man as I.*

"You're a brave lad, going up by yourself," the owner continued. "I love the Old Dame, but I've spent more than a few sleepless nights there."

"I'll be right," I said, full of confidence. *If your disguise is a weasel, your real self must be a monster. No wonder you couldn't hack it.*

"Righto, then."

The Charabanc only carried folk up the mountain when the chalet was open, so I rode up the winding dusty track on Dodger, my father's favourite horse. "You take good care of ol' Dodge and he'll take care of you," he'd said on our departure. "That horse has more sense than most folk." I'd bit my tongue, stopping myself from enquiring whether he had any horses that could hold a paintbrush. Now, with my shirt sticking to my sweaty back, I wondered if my father would be missing me or the horse more.

The last town was now far behind, and I marvelled at the beauty of the high country. As we gained altitude, wildflowers and wattle gave way to eucalypts, and the air was sweet, full of life. Wallabies pricked their ears as we approached, then scampered off between the trees. Flocks of colourful parrots chirped in delight, dancing between the branches. If anywhere in this sun-blasted continent could be called paradise, this was it. Grinning at the irony of being punished by a stint in such natural splendour, I renewed my vow to keep my end of the bargain.

The winding track provided majestic views of the valley. Through the trees, small plumes of smoke rose from the villages far below, and I wondered at the luck of those who were no doubt searching for gold. The rush was over, and nowadays all the mining was done by wealthy companies and desperate fools. With a smile, I climbed back on my weary horse, leaving the thoughts and failures of the miners far below.

* * *

Saddle-sore and weary, we arrived at the chalet, its pale-yellow weatherboards a welcome sight. After stabling Dodger, I strode up the granite steps, unlocked the wooden doors, and entered. She was marvellous; large sitting rooms, ample fireplaces, even a billiards room, but the Old Dame of the Mountain would keep me busy, sure enough. A lick of paint needed here, a dripping tap to fix there, and she'd be right as rain come winter. The perfect way to prove myself a man, to redeem myself for the damage done.

After finding the kitchen and heating a can of beans--not having the energy to prepare anything grander--I ate my fill, enjoying the simple meal amidst the natural beauty of the mountain and the splendour of the chalet. Reflecting upon how coming here to repair this glorious building was my punishment, I reminded myself to make sure I thanked my father for making this possible. Of course, it wasn't completely selfless on his behalf—his reputation would be tarnished if word got out about my misdeeds—but his intervention was very much appreciated.

With a candle lighting my way, I ascended the staircase to the second floor. There was a chill in the air, a draft coming through a window. My boots echoed down the dark and empty hallway as I entered room after room, searching for the source of the draft. Reaching the last room and finding the window closed, I turned around and walked back. The only room I hadn't checked was at the other end of the hall, at the top of the stairway.

The flame flickered with every step I took as I approached the final room, and the scent of eucalyptus—faint on the cool breeze—reached me. As I pushed open the door the flame went out, and I found myself in sudden darkness. Holding my breath, hearing nothing but the beat of my heart, I entered the room. My eyes adjusted to the dark and found the curtain concealing the open window. Trying to ignore the sensation of being watched, I crossed the room and slid the window shut with a satisfying thunk. I turned and left the dark room, and only exhaled after closing the door behind me.

In the hallway I re-lit the candle, the pinprick of light and heat warming my heart. I shook my head at my foolishness, there was no way I could have been watched as the curtain was closed. Selecting a room halfway down the hall, I pushed open the door and entered a room, bed already made up and a window looking out into the dark. Too tired to get undressed, I lay down and closed my eyes, taking comfort in the fact that I was truly alone. I blew out the candle and lay back on the bed, ready for sleep to come. *This will be the making of me.*

* * *

Laughter from the kookaburras woke me, and I smiled. After trotting downstairs in the dawn of a new day, I had my first proper look around the Old Dame. She was splendid, of course. From the magnificent ballroom to the dining room with its vaulted ceiling, there were oak panels, lavish furniture, and windows through which the most pristine views resided. The morning light also revealed things that needed work I'd missed the previous night; some cracked panelling, a spot of water damage, peeling paint. Nothing that couldn't be fixed with enough gumption and know-how. After breakfast and seeing to Dodger, I got started.

The sun beat down relentlessly as I sanded back the façade, sweat dripping from my brow. Niggling doubts crept in as my muscles cramped and ached. I may have been naïve about how hard this was going to be, yet was not about to renege on my promise; not about to let myself down, nor my father. Gritting my teeth, I stuck at the task.

When the screech of cockatoos filled the evening air, my blistered hands loosened their grip on the sanding block. *This is what it means to be a man, keeping your promises, paying for your mistakes.* I boiled some tea and ate dinner while watching the sun set. My hands and muscles ached, but I was content with having done a hard day's work.

Exhausted, I clambered into bed, ready for the dark to take me. I had barely closed my eyes when the heavens split with a monstrous cry, jolting me awake. An inhuman scream filled the air, followed by a growl as deep as the mountain's bones. *What the devil is out there?* Hands trembling, heart racing, I looked out the window. Pale moonlight fell on the majestic gorge, and a horrific cry echoed through the night; an ancient forbidding, a warning. Another sound reached me, the snorting and stamping of my terrified steed. *Dodger!* I had to help.

Torn between prayer and horror, wanting to save Dodger yet petrified, I knelt by the window, transfixed with fear. *Coward. Pathetic.* I took a steadying breath and tore myself from the aperture. Grabbing my knife from its sheath, I left the room and crept down the hall to the stairs. A thump came from the ceiling right above me. *It's inside!* A deep growl shook the chalet's foundations and my bowels turned to ice. If that thing was already inside, nothing was going to stop me from getting out.

THE CARETAKER

I lurched down the stairway, holding my breath, unable to make out the steps in the darkness. If I allowed myself to breathe, I would scream, my voice and soul joining the cacophony of terror. Steeling my resolve, I made my way through the lobby and stepped outside.

Alone and exposed in the moonlight, my skin crawled under the gaze of unknowable numbers of evil beady eyes. The distressed whinny of Dodger reached me above the demonic symphony. I had to go to him. Heart racing, I scarpered between trees, through rose bushes, knowing without any shred of doubt I was being pursued. I ran like a fiend to escape the demons pursuing me, and burst through the stable doors.

The horse was as scared as I; eyes wide, nostrils flared, kicking up a storm. Holding out my hand, I approached, hoping to calm the beast. "Easy, Dodger. Easy now." My voice came out as a creak, betraying my fear. Dodger twisted right and left, retreating to the rear of the stall. As I stepped closer, a *thump thump thump* came from the roof of the stable. Dodger whinnied in fright, spun and kicked the door of the stall clean off. A plank of wood struck me, knocking me against a sturdy beam. As I collapsed, Dodger bolted past, his hoofsteps sure as he launched into the night.

I prayed for the darkness to take me before the demons. I had yet to atone for my sins.

* * *

Melodic birdcalls roused me to a world of pain and confusion. With a wince, I touched my aching skull, and the scent of hay and manure brought back the horrors of the previous night. My hands scrabbled in the dirt for my knife and then I paused, gathering my wits. The songs of the lyrebirds and currawongs told me the danger had passed, that Dodger and I were safe. *Dodger!* I turned to the stall, hoping the brave steed had returned. It was vacant, and my heart sank. *Another victim of your cowardice.*

With a heavy heart, I returned to the chalet and broke my fast, sharing my toast with the boldest of the birds. *This is no place for the weak.*

The torn-up earth and flattened saplings left in Dodger's wake were easy enough to find. Hoping he'd managed to reach safety or shelter from the terrors of the night, I followed his trail. My eyes were focused on his tracks, but when the earth turned to granite, I knew where his mad dash had taken him. I stepped forward, raised my head, and opened my eyes. Clear blue sky above, green trees far, far below. Blinking against the wind, I turned from the gorge and wiped away useless tears.

Anger filled me as I returned to the Old Dame. I stamped up the stairs, searched through each room for any trace of the monsters from last night. I found nothing. Stepping into a bathroom, I got undressed and turned on the faucet. A groan from the pipes before a stream of icy water burst forth. With the pure mountain water, I cleaned the filth from my body, scoured my soul, and prepared my muscles and mind for the job at hand.

Refreshed and revitalised, I cracked open a paint tin and got to work.

* * *

The hours went by and soon a layer of fresh new paint covered the Old Dame's facade. Stepping back, I forced myself to smile. *This is work to take pride in.* Turning from the chalet, I looked to the red-tinged sky. A chill filled the air. Night would come soon, and this time I would be ready.

After a simple dinner, I went from room to room, closing each window tight and securing every door. Exhausted as I was, with my body and soul craving naught but rest, sleep still evaded me. A dripping tap echoed through the silence. *A task for the morrow.* Then a tapping—gentle at first—on a window. *Just the wind.* I closed my eyes. In my self-imposed darkness, I could see only the helpless maid as I held her down, could hear only her anguish. Pressing my hands to my ears, I tried to block out the sound, and it worked. Until a demonic wail cleaved the silence.

I shut my eyes tight, my heart hammering in my chest. A mournful cry from the horrid gorge scaled the granite cliffs, crept through the ghostly gums, slunk up the stairs, wormed through the floorboards and up the bedpost. Icy tendrils of mist wrapped around my arms, slid between my fingers and slipped into my ears, carrying the repulsive sound. Louder and louder grew the cry, penetrating deeper and deeper inside me, as if it were searching for the very core of my being. Fighting the horrid voice, I pulled my hands from my ears and jumped out of bed.

Banshee screams filled the air as I opened the door and stepped into the hall. Gripping my knife, I ran for the stairs, my only thought to escape the wretched building.

A thump came from the door at the end of the hall, stopping me in my tracks. Another blow threatened to burst the door off its hinges. I did not want to know what was on the other side.

Vaulting over the railing, I landed on the lower flight of the stairs, tripped and fell forward into the lobby. As I lay in a crumpled heap, the door upstairs burst open. *Move.* Ignoring the pain shooting through my body, I staggered to my feet. I took one step forward, then another. A blood-curdling cry filled the lobby and I was hurled back to the floor by some invisible force. Heart hammering, the taste of blood on my tongue, I braced myself to get up and run.

Before I could move, something cold wrapped around my leg. I tried to pull free, but couldn't budge. *Weak.* My leg burned with ice where the thing touched me, and the cold hand slid up further, up to my knee. Knife in hand, I twisted around, ready to sever the tentacle of ice and free my numb leg. But there was nothing. *It must be under your clothes.* With my hands shaking, frantic, I cut through the waistband of my pyjamas and forced the blade down the leg, cutting open the soft fabric. All I could see were the gashes I'd cut in my calf. As I stared at the blood in horror, the invisible tendril slid up further, up and around my thigh, up to my saddle-sore skin. *No no no!*

I tried to grab the invisible tentacle of ice, tried to pull it away, but it was as nebulous as a memory of violence and hate. The icy coil pushed inside me, and I cried out, unable to fight back. My nails dug into the floorboards as I tried to pull myself away, tried to escape, but a weight forced me down, held me in place as my anguish filled the room. As the invisible tendril squirmed and wormed deeper inside, tears streamed down my face and a guttural cry burst from my agonised soul.

The icy fingers inside me reached up through my guts to my heart, pierced into my core, wriggled deeper and deeper to the innermost heart of my being. My mind exploded in white hot agony. I no longer feared death, for I was already in hell.

* * *

The demons did not kill me, as that would have been a mercy. I awoke in a pool of blood in the lobby and pulled myself to my feet. Using a plank of wood for support, I staggered to the bath and drank my fill from the faucet as the water washed away most of the blood and filth.

With needle and thread, I stitched the deep gashes in my leg, then dashed alcohol over the wounds. The fire, wretched fire, brought the night before into barbaric clarity. I had to leave. *This is no place for the weak.* If redemption were ever possible for my sins, it was foolish to think I could earn it through some self-serving display.

Carrying what few miserable items I could, I locked the doors of the Old Dame behind me, leaving the blood to soak into the floor. *A job for the next caretaker.*

The trees erupted in a cacophony of mocking laughter. Even the kookaburras knew, as I knew, that to the marrow of my bones I was naught but cowardice hiding behind violence. I stopped in my tracks. If I was lucky enough to make it down the mountain, I'd never live down the shame of my failure. Returning without Father's favourite horse would be hard enough. Yet I could not endure another night of torment and horror. *Would it be better to never go home?*

I followed Dodger's path to the edge of the cliff, but was unable to look down, unwilling to see his wrecked body far below. All my learnings—all that could be taught by Englishmen—meant nothing under this unforgiving sun. The only thing I know for sure is the darkness in one's heart is no match for that hidden in the granite gorge, the cold heart of the mountain forged from stone and fire.

About the Author:

Austin P. Sheehan is a writer of speculative fiction, and lives on Wurundjeri Woi Wurrung country with his wife and their greyhounds.

Austin's debut novella 'Submerged City' was published by Deadset Press in 2019, and he has also had short stories published in Planet Scumm magazine, and in anthologies by Black Hare Press, Deadset Press, Scout Media, Fantasia Divinity, Blood Song Books and Zombie Pirate Publishing.

Find him on twitter @AustinPSheehan, go to www.austinpsheehan.com.

Australia's second oldest capital city must surely
be the home to more than a few ghosts.

RIVULET

Madeleine D'Este

The moon was a murky white disc, high in the sky resting on an eiderdown of clouds. She yanked her friend's front door closed and wrapped her knitted scarf around her neck once more.

Rain had fallen while they dissected their lives at the kitchen table, talking poetry, unrequited love and the sweet promises of tomorrow. At one a.m. on a wintry Wednesday, the town was abandoned to the whims of the night. Every curtain and every eyelid closed, everyone asleep but her.

Bolstered by a belly full of shiraz, capricciosa and Tim Tams, she surveyed the deserted street. With her keys clutched in her fist – her makeshift knuckle-duster – she set off home.

Her footsteps squelched over the glistening bitumen, and above her head, electricity crackled through moist pylon wires. She hunched her shoulders and walked with her legs wide apart, a deliberate macho gait designed to hopefully obfuscate.

Tyres sloshed on the wet road up ahead and she darted into a shop doorway. Out of the light, out of sight. She crammed herself into the deepest corner of the alcove as a blue sedan cruised past slowly. She waited and waited with breath held and burning lungs, until the faraway ping of the pedestrian crossing was the only sound.

Leaving the doorway with a grumble, she picked up her pace over the soggy leaf-scattered footpath. The straight strip of shops stretched down the Elizabeth Street hill into the dark and desolate heart of town. Overhead, raindrops thrummed on the iron awnings, dribbling out of downpipes into roadside gutters and through the clenched-teeth grates into the drains. Yellow streetlights dotted the road, like small ponds of safety, while in every other direction, tides of shadows encroached.

Behind grey-mirrored shop windows, blank-faced mannequin families watched her walk by and empty cash drawers sat like hungry mouths. Neon signs flashed in vain, crying out to invisible midnight shoppers.

Already halfway home, she crossed a small bridge where the built-up town opened to a steep sided drain. With banks of stone fashioned by convict toil this was where the dark waters of the hidden river trickled. The subterranean rivulet where black rats the size of small dogs lived, oiled like brilliantine.

Swelled by the night rains, the Hobart rivulet murmured. Its song, gurgling over the stones, bristled and teased her skin. It drew her closer, enticing her to peer into the depths, into the land that was. The country now forgotten, covered over by concrete, mobile phone shops and bus stops.

A splash of puddles interrupted the song and she darted back from the railing. A rumbling engine approached and headlights blossomed into the darkness. On the bridge she was exposed, no shop doorways to hide in. She hurried and huddled behind a bin, squeezing between the metal and the wall.

The same blue car ambled by.

Again she waited, biting on her knuckles, ignoring the stench of rubbish while her thighs whined with cramp. When all was dead quiet again, just the raindrops and the faraway crossing's comforting ping, she unwound herself and stamped the pins and needles from her feet.

She set off again. There were three more blocks to the flat she called home, above the Italian restaurant. A miserable drizzle settled in and she trudged on umbrella-less, droplets pearling on her fringe and chest. Three blocks was still too far to run.

A burglar alarm cried out in the distance as she crossed over the tiny river a second time. Again, the rivulet called to her, drawing her towards the water with its silvery, slippery song. The song deepened into chant of anguish, of estrangement, thick with a mother's disappointment. Her heart ballooned in her chest and she inched closer. A drain was not a place to play, even in the brightest daylight. Still she peered, nearer, deeper, into the blackness of the pipe under the road. Into the emptiness, the past, the land lost, maimed and enfeebled. What was once a river is now a trickle under the town, man-made scars built over blood-soaked soil.

Yet water stops for no one. Here, now, forever, water always finds a way. She stepped over the iron railing and down onto the worn cobbles.

A hand yanked at her elbow. She jerked and gasped, swivelling left and right. No one was there, only the night all around her. The unseen hand pulled at her foot and she skidded on the mossy stones. Again it pushed her, shunting her into the tunnel until the dark enveloped her. With her voice smothered in her throat, she lashed out with her house-key weapon, her blows striking nothing but air. Her back was shoved against the cold slimy tunnel wall, the breath pushed from her lungs.

A car pulled up beside the bridge. The same blue sedan. Her eyes bulged, breath rough and rapid in her nostrils. The man got out. He marched up and down beside the railing. A hooded raincoat hid his face as he retraced her footsteps from only seconds earlier. Her pulse thumped in her neck, his jerky strides chilling her blood.

When he finally gave up and disappeared from view, she exhaled and rested her head against the cold stone.

Then she glanced back into the dark tunnel and whispered into the gloom. "Thank you".

About the Author:

Madeleine D'Este is a Naarm-based (Melbourne) writer, podcaster and reviewer who spent her formative years wandering the streets of Nipaluna (Hobart) late at night. Inspired by folklore and forteana, D'Este writes dark mysteries, including steampunk, historical fantasy and vampire tales. Her novel The Flower and The Serpent was nominated for an Australian Shadow for Best Novel in 2019.

The magnificent wilderness in Tasmania's Huon
Valley is a great spot to go camping.
Just don't go alone.

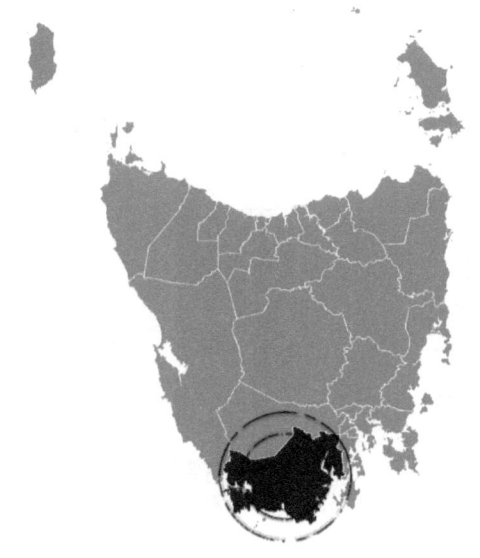

HERE KITTY KITTY

Eva Leppard

"It's my cat," said Elliana.

Frankie looked at the animal. He rubbed the bridge of his nose and squinted, readjusting his thick glasses. The animal squatted in front of them. Its coat shimmered, the late afternoon sun catching the grey and blue glimmers.

"It doesn't look like a cat to me."

Elliana put her hands on her hips and squared her jaw. "Mate, he's my cat," she repeated. "Are you telling me that I don't know my own cat?"

Frankie shrugged. "I didn't know that cats had feathers."

"Some do. He's rare."

"Ok." He didn't look convinced. The boy bent down to pat its head but withdrew his hand quickly, as if he had been burned. "Shit, is it supposed to have eyes like that?"

"His eyes," said Elliana with menacing quiet, "are fine."

The boy took a step back and glanced around. The afternoon sun was touching the top of the gum trees as it sank below the mountains.

"He's a big bugger."

"She's very well proportioned, actually," said Elliana. "This breed is always larger than other cats."

"Looks a bit like a platypus," he suggested.

"Have you ever seen a metre-long platypus with feathers and red eyes?" she asked

He admitted that he hadn't.

"And teeth?"

"No but to be fair I've never seen a cat that looks like that either."

"It sounds like you don't know that much about animals," said Elliana.

"Yeah ok. Anyway, I'd better be off."

"Already?" she said. "You just got here."

"The sun's going, and I don't want to be riding past your bit of river after dark. My Nanna says that the bunyip lives out here."

"Don't be a dickhead, there's no bunyip out here."

"That's not what my nanna said. She said people have always told stories of bunyips in this part of the Huon." He squinted behind him at the water in the distance, fringed by trees. "She said that your property is the starting point. That's why . . ." his voice trailed off and he rubbed at his face.

"That's why what?"

"Nothing."

"There's no bloody bunyip, ok? Don't you think I'd know about it?"

Elliana remembered a school trip up to Hobart a year or so ago, when they had gone to the museum and seen the ancient megafauna. Elliana and her classmates gazed in awe at the diprotodon.

"Think of it as a giant wombat," said the guide. "A giant wombat with big teeth."

"But not carnivorous?" said a girl, her voice hopeful.

"Yeah, imagine that thing chasing you down and ripping you apart," said a voice from the back, and an excited titter ran through the group.

"Shut up Max you dickhead," Elliana had said. "Look at those teeth. They're for grinding, not ripping."

"That's right," said the guide. "But does anyone know what mythological creature the Diprotodon is supposed to have given rise to?"

"Dragon?" said one boy.

The guide tilted her head to one side and squinted at him. "No-oo. Anyone else?"

"Godzilla?" said another.

The guide shot a stricken glance at their teacher for assistance.

He clapped his hands to get the group's attention. "An Australian mythological animal."

"Bunyip," said one of the older girls, rolling her eyes. "The stories say they live in billabongs and waterholes and drags people to their deaths."

"That's right," said the guide.

"If there was a bunyip out here don't you think I'd know about it?" Elliana repeated.

Frankie shrugged again and frowned at the animal that sat in front of him, staring off into the distance.

"Maybe. I dunno. Are you coming to school this week? Miss Bailey says she'll ring your mum if you don't come back soon."

"Mum's sick," said Elliana. "So it would be no good Miss Bailey sticking her nose in anyway."

Frankie rode off, puffs of dust flurrying behind him as he peddled away. The sunlight tinged his hair red as he disappeared out of sight.

He could move quickly for a little bloke.

"Come on Jelly Meat," Elliana said to her cat.

She squatted down and touched his back. His body shuddered, as if there was a current running through him.

"What's the matter? Are you ok?"

A noise rose up in the distance, from where the serpentine murky water splayed out over the paddock. The Huon River was expansive in some areas, but here, water had flowed out of it many years ago, pooling into a waterhole on the property. A low howling grew to a wavering crescendo which cut off abruptly, although the noise continued to hang in the air for a few moments. Jelly Meat rose up on his thick legs and lifted her head, sniffing the air, her elongated face waving gently back and forth, red tinged eyes half closed. A low rumble came from his belly, and Elliana wrapped her arms around him and picked him up. A damp smell rose from the fur that ran under the creature's feathers, and Ellaina shouldered her way through the screen door into the darkening, silent house. Jelly Meat waggled his behind to be put down as the door clicked shut behind them and she placed him down on the lino, bending to give him a gentle kiss on the head before he disappeared into the gloom of the kitchen.

Frankie was an idiot. Of course Jelly Meat was a cat. Dad had told her so, years ago, the night that he carried Jelly Meat home after finding him with his foot caught in a rabbit trap. Her father had told her to look after him, to nurse him back to health, until he was well enough to head back out into the wilderness.

But then Dad had shot through and Jelly Meat had healed but the right time to let him go had never come. And now he was all that she had.

Elliana stood in the empty house, listening for any noise. The TV wasn't on, nor the radio, and the hum of the fish tank filled the room. She didn't know why she left the filter going; the fish were long dead.

But sometimes it was the only comforting sound that she could hear.

She pulled some two-minute noodles down from the shelf, filled a bowl with water and upended the packet into it. The water had a brown tinge to it, thanks to the burst of rain last night. "Just enough to wash the possum poo into the gutters," mum would have said.

Maybe mum would be home soon.

Perhaps.

She watched the glow of the microwave for, as she always thought grudgingly, four minutes. Pushing the empty bottles that lined the wall under the sink out of the way, she reminded herself to put the recycling bin out.

There was a snuffling in the hallway as Jelly Meat nosed along the wall, finding his way in the darkness. He was fidgety tonight, pacing back and forth along the corridor, his belly low to the ground and his side brushing against the peeling wallpaper. There was a scratching noise as his feathers caught on the fraying flocked green flakes that had once been a wall of lush leaves and branches, some catching in his whiskers as he leaned against the wall.

He pushed his head against the fly screen door and opened it into the night. It was full dark now, the low moon just rising in the east, its hook hung heavy against the distant mountains that hugged the horizon. The microwave beeped behind Elliana as she followed Jelly Meat outside.

The keening noise rose up again from the far paddock, and the cat replied, in a strange, never heard before voice. Before she could take hold of him, he slipped down the steps and cut his way through the long grass of the front paddock faster than she had ever seen him move.

"Jelly Meat," she called after him, her voice piercing the night, but he ignored her. After closing the screen door behind her, Elliana ran after him.

When she was little, very little, she hadn't been allowed anywhere near the river. It was too dark, too deep. There had been too many fences for her to get through. Now, she could easily climb, and there was no one to stop her anyway. Jelly Meat had a good start on her, but she knew where he was heading and didn't need to follow the same path, under broken fences and bent barbed wire. She pulled herself over the metal gates and wooden stiles until the lights of the house twinkled far away in the distance and the dark smell of the waterhole filled the air.

The river was a tourist attraction in some places, picturesque and expansive, but here it was stagnant and boggy, with dead gum trees jutting out of the still dark water.

59

There was a rustling to Elliana's side and Jelly Meat appeared, roughly bumping his thick body against her leg. She dropped her hand to caress his head, and as she did so a noise rose from the swamp in front of her. A high, keening cry that hung in the air for a moment. Something huge flew overhead. An owl. Its wings rustled the hair on the top of her head. How big could an owl grow?

Crouching down, she wrapped her arms around Jelly Meat's neck.

The quarter moon illuminated a ripple emanating from the surface of the water, a slow, lazy undulation that made the moon's reflection jerk. A noise came from the bush that bordered the river, the gumtrees that stretched all the way to the Hartz Mountains. She had always been told not to go there, not to walk into those trees because they didn't stop and once you were deep enough, chances were that no one would find you until your bones were bleached white from the elements-if the Tassie devils left anything of you at all.

The sound of something crashing through the dark trees took all her attention, but she noticed that under her hands Jelly Meat was thrumming and bristling.

Elliana felt very, very small.

"Come on," she said, wrapping her arms around his neck and pulling him close. "Let's go. Let's go home." She turned her head to find the warmth and safety of her house, but a mist covered the yellow glow of home, hiding the only guide she had.

She pulled her animal's neck again, but Jelly Meat was as solid and as immovable as a boulder. A noise that she had never heard pulsed deep within him.

Although she was looking down, trying to shift her cat, she noticed a change in the nature of light around her. A sickening greenish glow diffused the mist. She thought the mist itself was changing, but then realised something else was rising up from the ground, a vapour with tendrils that wound gently around her limbs. Before her brain registered what was happening, she felt a sharp tug around her ankles and gripped Jelly Meat's neck tighter to stop herself falling forwards.

The movement on the water had stopped, but the sounds from the surrounding trees were more purposeful, the cracking of low lying bushes and the snapping of twigs in the gum trees metres above her.

Her feet grew numb, as if the cold and the mist was swallowing her senses. "Help me Jelly Meat." Dogs could do amazing feats of bravery; pulling their owners out of quicksand or from burning buildings – was there any reason that her cat couldn't do the same?

"Let's go home," she said as electricity bristled inside him. "Come on boy."

61

Her legs couldn't move at all, the malaise that had fallen over them now eddied up through her body. With a thrill of joy, she felt Jelly Meat stand up and lurch forwards, her arms around his neck not hindering his movements. "Yes boy," she cried, not minding that her voice was shaking because the ground was moving. "That's it, good job!"

In the sick light that hung over them, Jelly Meat glowed the same colour as the mist; his feathers and the fog mirroring each other in a strange symbiosis.

Her body slid over the damp grass, and she twisted her head to look behind them, the light of the house now low and hidden by the mist.

She tugged on Jelly Meat's neck. "Good job boy. Now turn around, let's head towards the lights."

Instead, she slid closer to the black maw of the water that spread out in front of her. 'Not this way,' she sad to him, her arms clinging to him. 'Not towards the water, home!'

The dark water was rippling from the vibrations that shook the ground and something dark was blocking out the stars. The scrape of Jelly Meat's strange prehensile feathers against her bare arms triggered something in her, and Ellainia had a blazing burst of clarity and understanding. Of course Jelly Meat wasn't a cat! Everything was so, so crystal clear, and for one giddying moment she felt utterly grown up and wise.

She couldn't feel her body at all now. A soporific detachment washed over her. The mist was already digesting her, but of course she didn't know that. As Elliana was dragged into the dark water, the last thing she saw was the rictus face of her parents, waiting for her just below the surface.

About the Author:

Eva Leppard lives in lutruwita (Tasmania) with an elegantly sufficient amount of children and a disturbingly large number of rescue animals, all of which she raised by hand whether they liked it or not. She writes fantasy and occasionally science fiction (usually by accident), and her debut novel The Pitfalls of Being a Goddess will be published by Between the Lines Publishing in late 2022.

For updates, head to https://justevastories.com/

The Australian Capital Territory has more monsters per square meter than any other state or territory.

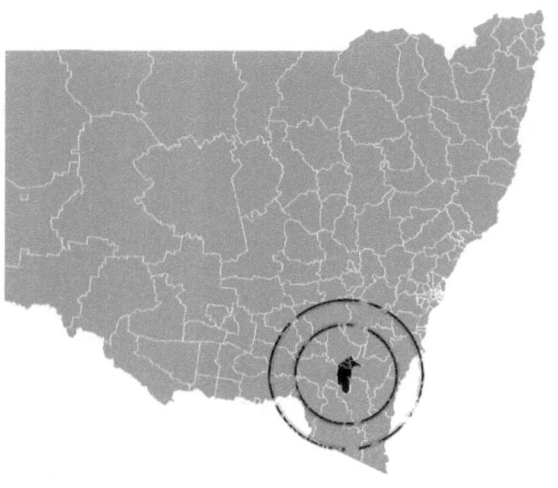

SIGN ME UP

Emily Wrayburn

Natasha jumped as the burner phone vibrated in her pocket. She reached for it, casting a furtive glance over her shoulder as she fumbled to answer.

"Hello?"

Three numbers were programmed into the phone, but none had real names saved against them. Natasha was never sure whose voice she was about to hear when a call came through.

"Natasha. It's Harry. Are you alone?"

Harry Weatherall. Natasha still couldn't believe she was in communication with the public face of and the money behind Tipping the Scales, the national dragon rescue network. The borderline illegal, some would say "terrorist", network. She always put that thought out of her mind.

"Harry, hi! I'm alone. I mean, sort of. I've just left work. I'm walking through the car park."

"Talk to me until you reach your car. How was your day?"

"Same as always. We sent the latest report up to the Executive this afternoon."

"That's good for us to know. Have you reached your car?"

Natasha tucked the phone under her chin while she searched for her car key. "One more second." After finding her keys, she unlocked the car and slid into the driver's seat, then switched on the ignition to get the heater running. She'd spotted a sprinkling of snow on the tops of the Brindabellas that morning. Despite rumours that it sometimes snowed at ground level in the city, the dustings on the peaks in the national parks were all she'd ever seen in her eight years in Canberra.

"Okay," she said. "What's going on?"

"How do you feel about going out in the field tonight?"

"I . . . what? I'm not . . . Why me?"

"We need an extra pair of hands and there aren't many available to get to Canberra at short notice. You're already here. Do you remember the report about the Ice Breather nesting near Perisher?"

"The one they wanted to get rid of before the ski season opened?"

"That's her. Don't want an overprotective dragon mama in your ski fields when thousands of tourists are about to descend, do you?"

It would be spectacular, Natasha thought. "They certainly wouldn't."

Natasha remembered the report Harry referred to. An Ice Breather this far north was unusual. She'd settled in one of the colder parts of the region, but it was still warmer than the dragon breed preferred, especially when they were nesting.

"The X is scheduled for next week, so we've been trying to move her on. She got one of our guys right in the chest last night and I can tell you, her ice breath hasn't suffered despite her location. We can't afford to miss a night trying to get her to leave so it'd be a real help if you could come out with us."

"X" was short for "extermination" and it was how Harry and the rest of Tipping the Scales referred to the dragon culls that the Government department Natasha worked for organised. Up until now, Natasha's entire role had been to send intel through to Harry and his people. She'd never had any inkling she'd end up in the field.

"I *can* come," Natasha said. "But I won't know what I'm doing. I don't want to screw it up for you."

"You've had your training."

"That was one weekend."

"You learned everything you needed to. I promise. And you'll have some of our best people with you. What do you say?"

67

Natasha paused. She'd never seen a dragon in the wild before. This would be a fantastic chance, and she'd be helping rescue it at the same time. On the other hand, if anyone from work found out . . . Leaking the odd report to TTS was one thing. Taking part in a dragon rescue mission was quite another.

She took a breath. "I'll do it."

"Fantastic. Get home and rug up as warm as you can and have something to eat. I'll send someone to meet you at Poet's Corner in Civic at six-thirty. They'll be using the codes we taught you."

"Poet's Corner?"

"You know, the open-air place with the statues? Near the comic shop."

Natasha couldn't place the statues but knew the comic shop so she figured she could find it easily enough. "All right. I'll be there."

"Beautiful! Good luck!" Harry terminated the call before Natasha had a chance to even consider changing her mind.

* * *

All the way home, Natasha wondered if she was making a mistake. In the end, she kept coming back to the drone footage on YouTube of one of the government exterminations. The poor dragon had put up a good fight, but he'd become tangled in the net dropped from a helicopter. The image of the beast struggling went through Natasha's head every time she sent a report of a confirmed dragon location to her superiors. She hated it, but a job was a job. When her previous role had been found surplus to requirements, she'd been redeployed to this one. Joining Tipping the Scales made it a little more bearable while she tried to find work elsewhere, and Harry had remarked more than once that the intel she provided was a great asset to the group. She still felt a warm glow in her chest when she remembered the first time he'd thanked her over the phone, gushing about how much work they'd be able to do with the information she'd passed on.

That was why she knew that she was making the right decision tonight. TTS's work was important, and if her presence was required to ensure the mission could continue, then she would be there.

Two hours later, clothed in thermals, a thick coat, a beanie and gloves, Natasha arrived in Civic and located the statues Harry had mentioned. For a few minutes, she sat on one of the nearby benches, drumming her fingers on one knee and jiggling her leg. Then she stood, pacing around the area, keeping an eye out for someone who might be another dragon enthusiast. She returned to the statues and was reading the plaque underneath the bust of a poet named Judith Wright when a hand on her arm made her jump.

"Nice night for music," the man said in a low voice.

For a moment, Natasha forgot the code she'd been taught, and wondered what the man was on about. Then the reply came to her. "I've got to practise my scales."

"My concerts always crash and burn," the man agreed, grinning. "Natasha?" She nodded. "I'm Dominic."

"Good to meet you," Natasha said, though it sounded almost like a question with a squeak on the last syllable. Suddenly it was real. This man, whom she'd never met before, was going to take her on a risky flight out to the mountains, where she could be attacked by an angry dragon. And if word got back to her bosses, she'd lose her job.

"The car's not far. Let's go," Dominic said, all business.

He turned and started walking but Natasha was frozen to the spot. What was she doing?

"Dominic, I . . ." she began, but when he turned around with an expectant expression on his face, she knew she couldn't back out.

"Coming," she said, and jogged a little to catch up to him.

They drove in silence so Natasha took the time to gather her thoughts. In the short time she had been at home, she had found the notebook from the Tipping the Scales training weekend, where she received a crash course in TTS field operations. The training had been non-stop, teaching them how to set off flares and harness themselves into a helicopter in order to lean out of the doors during a flight. Natasha had scribbled down everything she could remember in case she ever needed it again.

They'd spent the first morning sitting in a circle in Harry's expansive living room while they learned the basics. The key thing about TTS missions was that it was too dangerous to try to get close to a dragon, so the crews returned to dragon resting sites night after night, harassing the dragon until it decided to leave. If everything went to plan, there would be no dragon at the site a week or two later when the government exterminators showed up.

"And if they leave, will they go far enough?" someone had asked.

Harry nodded. "Research shows that if their territory is threatened to the point where they leave, they will put as much distance between them and the threat as possible. Of course, we have no way of tagging them to monitor that, so we have to hope for the best."

"It's a lot of effort for 'hope for the best'," someone else remarked.

"I'd rather make the effort than not, wouldn't you?"

Harry sent them outside for the lesson in flare ignition soon after. When someone asked if the flares were ever spotted by observers on the ground or in other aircraft during the mission, and whether the organisation ever got in trouble, their instructor had shrugged.

71

"Harry takes care of complaints about that sort of thing."

"How?"

The trainer cocked an eyebrow. "With his money." That was all she said on the matter, and she distracted everyone by thumping the bottom of the flare, igniting it.

Natasha closed her notebook when Dominic pulled off the highway and onto a gravel road. He pulled over and punched a code into a keypad and a gate opened ahead of them. Before them was a large, concreted area with a helicopter at one end. Dominic parked the car and he and Natasha disembarked.

"Leave your stuff in here," Dominic instructed. "We'll have everything we need up there."

As they crossed the tarmac, a person wearing black under a hi-vis vest was doing checks on the helicopter. Two others stood nearby. Dominic led Natasha over to them.

One of the figures turned as they approached. "Here she is!"

Butterflies swirled in Natasha's stomach. She'd met him on the training weekend, but it hadn't cured the awe she felt every time she thought about the work Harry enabled.

"Just keep it cool," she whispered to herself.

"Natasha, good to see you again!" Harry said, beaming at her. Then he turned to his companion. "Michaela, this is Natasha. She'll be taking Rob's spot tonight."

Michaela shook Natasha's hand, smiling. "We haven't got much time, but I want to give you a quick refresher before we leave." She picked up a bucket so full it sloshed water over the sides. In her other hand, she carried two flares. "Let's just run you through the basics."

Natasha nodded and was glad she'd reviewed her notes. Michaela led her over to the edge of the tarmac and set the bucket down. She talked through the process of setting off the flare, miming the actions as she did. When she was done, she handed the flare to Natasha and nodded. Natasha held it out in front of her and went through the motions a few times, talking herself through it in her head. *Line up the arrows until they click. Punch the end. Swap hands—don't hold the hot part.*

She took a breath and did it again for real. She'd known it was coming but still she yelped as the flare ignited and warmed beneath her hand. As she moved it to the other hand, she coughed, the smoke catching in her throat before the wind had the chance to carry it away. As the flare burned out, she relished the warmth it emanated before dropping it in the waiting bucket of water.

Michaela watched her detonate a second one just to be sure she knew what she was doing, then she nodded again, satisfied. "All right. You good to get yourself set up in the chopper?"

Natasha nodded, full of apprehension.

"Great. Let's go."

Natasha was harnessed when Dominic joined them a few minutes later, climbing up into the cockpit. Michaela fitted Natasha with headphones and microphone and then pulled her own over her ears.

"Just waiting for the all-clear," Dominic's voice came through the headset. He went through the pre-flight checks, then the helicopter gave a shudder as Dominic started the engine. The shriek of the helicopter's engine penetrated through Natasha's heavy headset. A minute later, the helicopter rocked back and forth from tail to nose as it took to the air. Natasha's stomach lurched and she took a deep breath to keep the queasiness at bay.

To stave the feeling off, she focused on seeing her first real-life wild dragon. She remembered everything she knew about Ice Breathers, how they had evolved for the cold climate, sucking in snow and ice, letting it accumulate in a chamber near their diaphragms until they expelled it again. The target could be buried in a snowdrift if they didn't get away in time.

They hadn't travelled very long when they passed over Canberra. As they passed over Lake Burley-Griffin, the water reflected the lights on the foreshore and the stars in the sky. Parliament House passed by underneath soon after. In the next few minutes, the lights became sparse as the suburbs gave way to national parks.

"It's about three-quarters of an hour's flight to the site," Dominic said. "She's built her nest in a valley between two peaks. Not the easiest spot to manoeuvre through but we've managed it the last couple of nights."

As they flew, Michaela ran Natasha through what she'd be doing. They'd each take a door, and Dominic would advise them when he was flying into the wind, so they could light their flares without the smoke obscuring his view.

Finally, Dominic announced that they were approaching the nest site. He circled low. Michaela got out of her seat and went to the window on her side of the cabin, so Natasha stood, too. Michaela made the walk look easy, but Natasha stumbled before she could grab onto the handrail near the door.

She peered through the glass and her breath caught. The dragon was below them.

The Ice Breather stared up at them, eyes glinting in the bright light. She bared her teeth and stretched her wings out to their full length. Puffs of vapour emerged from her nose. Drone footage could never capture the litheness of a dragon's neck, or the way their wings appeared translucent under the helicopter lights.

"I've got the recording ready," Dominic told them. "If you open the doors now, in another ten or fifteen seconds, we'll go."

Cold air stung Natasha's face as she pulled the door open. The helicopter's lights illuminated the snow and sludge on the mountainside below. She was wearing plenty of warm clothing, but the cold sneaked its way under the fabric regardless, little pinpricks of ice against her skin. She swallowed and held fast to the guardrail, waiting for instructions.

"This will be loud," Michaela warned.

Natasha nodded but she had no time to prepare herself before Dominic activated the recording of the high-pitched screech of a dragon's attack cry, blasting it through speakers mounted on the outside of the helicopter.

"Flares!" Michaela called.

Natasha pulled one out of her jacket pocket. She curled her arm through the guardrail so she could use both hands to line up the mechanism, then bashed the end of the flare on the outside of the helicopter. It roared to life, the smoke billowing behind them.

As the helicopter swooped downwards, the dragon rose to her hind legs and snapped at them, head thrashing as the smoke engulfed her.

Once the flare had died down, Natasha dropped the casing, letting it find a home in the snow to cool down. Dominic turned the chopper around and headed back for a second pass. The noise from the speakers blared again, compounded by the real dragon's cries below.

They dove close to the dragon again and Michaela and Natasha let off another pair of flares. Once they were past the nest, Dominic slowed the helicopter and turned off the dragon recording. Natasha swallowed and took a moment to catch her breath, loosening her grip on the guard rail, and flexing her fingers a few times to get the blood flowing again.

"Any movement?" Michaela asked.

"Not that I can see," Dominic replied, then, "Oh, no, hang on. She's on her way."

The attack cry came again, but this time the sound wasn't coming through the speakers. When Natasha leaned out the door, the dragon was in full flight. It would have been a majestic sight if she hadn't been coming right for them, her eyes blazing in the helicopter's headlights.

Dominic revved the engine, turning them to face the dragon. He turned on the recording again and then warned, "Hold on to your stomachs."

Natasha didn't know what that meant but it sounded dangerous, so she pulled herself inside. The helicopter plunged downward and her stomach lurched, only catching up to the rest of her a moment later. Once the helicopter was flying level again, she stuck her head outside and watched, wide-eyed, as they sped underneath the dragon and then out from under her tail.

By the time Dominic turned around, the dragon had done the same. Natasha held her breath as they tore towards each other.

"Dominic . . ." she squeaked, desperate to know that he had a plan.

But if he did, he was too late to act on it.

The dragon opened her mouth wide and a flurry of ice and snow spewed forth towards them. Dominic jerked the helicopter to the side but not quite fast enough; Natasha's side of the cabin took the brunt of the blast. She lost her grip on the handrail and was flung back towards her seat. Her head cracked against the headrest and whipped forward. She groaned, yanking off her headset to silence Dominic's string of profanities in her ear.

As Dominic pulled them back on course, Michaela swore from where she'd fallen on the other side of the cabin.

Natasha refitted her headset so she could communicate with the others and pulled herself up, wincing at the pain in her hip and backside. She was going to have some nasty bruises tomorrow. She made her way over to Michaela and held out a hand.

"You okay?" she asked.

"Damn it," Michaela replied. "That hurt." She grabbed Natasha's hand, and hauled herself up. "All right, Dom? What's happening?"

The helicopter had slowed right down. Dominic focused the headlights on the dragon's nest. The dragon was fussing around her egg.

"Come on," Michaela muttered. "Pick it up and get out of here."

A minute ticked by and Natasha started to think they hadn't been successful. But then the glint of scales caught in the headlight as the dragon took flight.

"She's got the egg," Dominic confirmed. Natasha wasn't sure how he could tell, but she took his word for it. "She's out of here. Heading south."

"Good," Michaela replied, and then added in a softer voice, "Get out of here, sweetheart. Go somewhere they'll treat you better. Or, better yet, where there aren't any humans to bother you at all."

They watched in silence for a few minutes until they could no longer see the dragon's scales illuminated in the headlights.

Michaela took a deep breath and shook herself. If Natasha wasn't mistaken, Michaela's eyes were a little misty. Natasha didn't mention it.

"Okay," Michaela said. "Take us home, Dom."

"Roger."

For a while no one said anything. Natasha stared through the window, even though there was little to see in the darkness. She tried to slow her breathing.

"How are you feeling?" Michaela asked.

In reply, Natasha held up one hand to show how it was shaking now that she had nowhere to focus her adrenaline. She grinned and Michaela returned the expression.

"Just be warned, you will crash so hard tonight," Michaela said. "Get Dominic to drop you at home. Go back to the collection point in the morning to get your car."

They landed back where they had started. Harry was waiting for them. "How did we go?" he asked, a hand out to help Natasha down to the tarmac. Now she was standing on them, her legs were like jelly. She leaned on Harry until she could support herself.

"We did it," she said breathlessly.

"Well done!" Harry's eyes were shining. "I knew you had it in you."

"I didn't." A hysterical giggle rose in Natasha's throat and burst out of her. She swayed on her feet and Harry took her by the shoulders, giving her a broad smile.

"Time for you to go home to bed," Harry said. "We'll debrief tomorrow." He guided her towards Dominic's car.

Natasha turned around, looking for Michaela. She was trailing behind, talking to Dominic.

"Michaela, thanks for getting me through tonight," Natasha said.

Michaela nodded in acknowledgement. "You did a great job. Maybe we'll see you again."

"I hope so."

Michaela smiled. "Goodnight Natasha."

Soon enough, Dominic was driving back onto the main road, Natasha in his passenger seat. He tuned the radio to a classical music station and Natasha let the music wash over her as she leaned her head against the window. The next thing she knew, Dominic was shaking her by the shoulder to wake her up. They were entering Canberra again, the lights of the northern-most suburbs twinkling as they drove down the Federal Highway.

"You're going to need to tell me how to find your place," he said.

"Right," Natasha said, shaking her head to clear it. She told him where to turn off the main road and then directed him through the suburbs until they reached her street.

When she reached her flat, she had no energy to change her clothes, so she just pulled off her jacket and outermost layers and flopped into bed in her thermals. She was asleep within a minute.

* * *

"Natasha, can I see you in my office?"

Natasha gulped. "Sure."

She stood and followed her boss, Stuart, into his office. He closed the door behind them, motioning for her to sit at the meeting table across from his desk. Her stomach churned as she took her seat.

"Did you have a good weekend?" Stuart asked, his back to her as he did something on his computer. Natasha tried to work out if it was a trick question. Did he know? Was he trying to bait her into admitting where she'd been? Or was it an innocent question? She racked her brain, trying to think of anything else she might be called into Stuart's office to discuss.

"Um," she finally said. "Yeah, it was fine. Didn't do much. You?"

"Oh, you know, bit busy," Stuart replied, then pushed his chair back so that Natasha could see his computer screen. "Anything you'd like to tell me, Natasha?"

Natasha stared at the high-resolution photo on the screen. It showed her leaning out of the helicopter, about to strike a flare on the outer shell. She hadn't realised she'd been grinning like that.

"How . . ." The rest of the sentence died in her throat. Her mouth had turned dry and the words wouldn't come out.

"Someone was flying a drone over the Snowys on Friday night. They thought we might want to know about the people disturbing a dragon we had marked for termination. Imagine my surprise when I saw your face in some of the photos."

Natasha wanted to say something. Deny it was her in the photo. Defend herself. Defend the dragons. Tell him that this entire government policy was wrong. But her throat was constricted. All she could do was take a shaky breath.

"What happens to me now?"

"As I'm sure you're aware, this is a serious breach of our code of conduct. Your termination papers have already been signed by the director. Your dismissal is effective immediately. You have until the end of the day to clear your things and leave."

"Thank you," she said, nodding. It seemed like the professional thing to say, even though she hadn't the slightest idea what she was thanking him for. She stood and walked out of Stuart's office, determined to leave with her head held high. Helping the dragon had been the right thing to do. She wouldn't regret that.

Packing up didn't take long. She hadn't personalised her desk so she only needed to remove a mug and jar of instant coffee from her drawer and stuff them into her bag. With one last glance around the office, she walked out, not stopping to say goodbye to anyone.

The knowledge that she was now jobless was yet to hit her, and all she could think as she walked out into the sunshine was that she was glad to be leaving the job she hated. Her one regret was that she hadn't been able to leave on her own terms.

That feeling changed over the next few days when she had to start explaining to people that she'd been fired. It didn't get any easier facing each shocked expression and answering the exclamations of "Oh my god, what happened?" even if she did answer with "I don't want to talk about it."

A week later she was drowning her sorrows in a mug of hot chocolate at a café in the city. She'd chosen an outdoor table underneath one of the tall gas heaters and took a perverse pleasure from the heat beating down on the back of her neck. She knew she'd have to be careful with money until she found a new job but after such a rotten week, she deserved a little treat.

A shadow fell over the table and she looked up. When she recognised the figure standing over her, she scowled. "What are you doing here?"

"May I?" Without waiting for an answer, Harry Weatherall pulled out the seat across from her and sat. Natasha went back to stirring her hot chocolate.

"How have you been?" he asked.

"How do you think?"

"Natasha, I want to apologise. The photos that were sent to your director . . . they were sent by someone else we thought was working for us. We have contacts dotted all through the government, as you know but . . . turns out this one was a double agent."

Natasha looked up. "Who was it?" In her mind she went through a list of her former colleagues, trying to remember if she'd ever witnessed any suspicious behaviour.

"That doesn't matter," said Harry. "I feel responsible, so I'd like to offer you compensation."

"What kind of compensation?" What could Harry offer her that would help her situation? She wouldn't say no to a decent amount of money. The longer she could stretch her savings the better.

"I'd like to offer you a permanent position with Tipping the Scales if you'd be willing to take it. You've done good work for us, and you know how impressed Michaela and Dominic were with your first flight. You won't have to go out in the field all the time if you don't want to. There's admin and other desk work at our offices, just like any other. Or we could train you up if you did want to be out there more. It's up to you. We'd love to have you."

Natasha swallowed. Harry made it all sound so straightforward. That was how she'd ended up on the mission in the first place. It was so easy to nod and go along with whatever he said. But did she want to work for TTS full time? Sure, saving the dragons from extermination was important to her, but could she commit to an organisation that walked the fine line between legal and illegal?

She looked back down at her hot chocolate.

Harry stood up, clearing his throat. "I'll let you think about it for a bit. There's no rush of course." He slid something into the centre of the table. When he removed his hand, she saw it was a sim card in a small plastic bag. "The first number on here will reach me. Shall I leave it with you?"

Natasha didn't reply but closed her own hand over the sim. Even if she didn't take the job, she wouldn't betray Harry's trust. The new number would be safe with her even if she decided not to take him up on his job offer. She glanced up at Harry and nodded. He returned the nod and left her alone.

She gulped down the rest of her hot chocolate and settled her bill. As she walked back to the Canberra Centre car park, her mind travelled back and forth between the memory of the captured dragon on YouTube and the one she had helped to save. She remembered the wide grin on her face in the photo on Stuart's computer screen. It had been exhilarating, and the result had been worth it. Harry said she could do that more often.

Who was she kidding? She didn't need time to think about it. If she called him now, Harry might still be nearby and they could discuss the particulars of the new job.

She sat down on a bench near the escalators and pulled out both the sim card and her TTS phone. Sliding the back cover off the phone, she swapped out the sim cards and turned the phone back on. As soon as the home screen loaded, she called the first number listed in the contacts.

Harry answered after two rings. "Hello, Natasha. That was quick."

"I've made my decision."

"I hoped it wouldn't take too long. Will you be joining us?"

"Absolutely, Harry," she said. "Sign me up."

About the Author:

Emily lives and works on Ngunnawal and Ngambri country. Her modern-day retelling of the Nutcracker was featured in the 2019 anthology "Christmas Australis" and is now book one of the Drosselmeier Industries series of fairy tale retellings available online.

In her non-writing life, she has a Masters of Museum and Cultural Heritage studies and works as a reference librarian. She has also studied drama and commits a lot of her time to local choirs and community theatre productions.

The New South Wales outback is dry and inhospitable, a place where only the hardy survive.

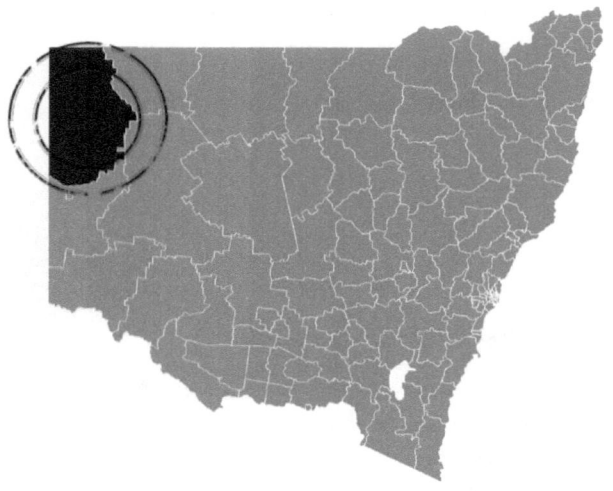

SALTBUSH BLUE

Faran Silverton

The noise in my head went quiet the first time I met Kody, in the shade of a bull sculpted out of spanners and harvester parts. His long fingers danced across scrap-metal as he shaped it into a magpie. After a while he glanced at me, raising one hand to sign, "Hello."

I fumbled, searching for the right words in his language. "Hello, I am Mia," I fingerspelled my name, the way I'd learnt years ago at school in Hobart.

We grinned at each other. Me, who liked to take things apart and put them back together as they should've been, and this man who liked to take things apart then make them into something else altogether. I hadn't known it then, in his stall at our annual field day, but Kody—with his face of blue skies and sun—would become the love of my life and father of my child.

Now, four years later, as he's about to head out for a morning of fixing fences in the back paddocks, he's frowning at the grey horse standing beside me in our house yard.

"Take the dirt bike," he signs.

"Maxie is fine," I say. The horse is way quieter than a motorbike and doesn't need fuel.

Evie watches us from the passenger side of Kody's ute, drumming her heels against the booster seat. Like any toddler, patience is not one of her strengths. So far there's no sign she's inherited my sensitivity to people, thank God. Experiencing other people's emotions is one problem I don't know how to fix for myself, let alone anyone else.

The furrow in Kody's brow deepens, but after a moment he shrugs and signs, "Be careful," even though he doesn't know where I'm going, what I'm doing, or who will be there. He never does, and he never asks. "I love you," he adds, folding me into a goodbye embrace.

I grin. "Me too."

* * *

The car sits askew on the shoulder, driver's door open, white paint stark against a palette of saltbush-gripped red dirt.

I shift in my saddle, reins loose on Maxie's neck, shading my eyes so I can see the young man staring at the car's engine. If he can't even figure how to prop the bonnet open, he's got Buckley's of working out why the car broke down. He drops the bonnet and paces, peering at his phone, holding it to his ear then stabs his finger at the screen. I snort. No amount of staring and swearing will magic up telephone service out here.

Nope, from here it's saltbush and dirt all the way to the nothingness of outback New South Wales shifting into South Australia, where the summer sun bakes the uneven road into a shimmer from one edge of the skyline to the other.

There's nothing here except the man and his white car. And me.

I'd put money down that it's not even his car. That whoever took it to the Western Sydney garage on its service sticker is still 1200 kilometres away, wondering what the hell happened to their old Commodore. They'd never guess it's just now given up the ghost on a deserted road somewhere north of Broken Hill.

I can't see the service sticker from where I've reined in my horse in on the hillside, but I saw it two days ago when the man pulled into the local roadhouse to get fuel. He swiped black curls off his face as he strutted into the café in his perfectly white shoes. He leant one gym-junkie arm on the counter, spreading his arrogance like grease on water, smiling at the girl who took his order with a smarm which grown men should never, ever inflict on fourteen-year old girls. Or anyone else.

He didn't see me propped against the workshop wall with my arms crossed over my grimy overalls, narrowing my gaze at him. His expensive clothes clashed with the beat-up Commodore he'd driven into the servo. Red road dust layered the undercarriage and locusts speckled the front grille. They were eating their way through the cropping country back east; a creeping plague you wouldn't believe unless you saw it. Not much different to this bloke with his car boot full of cash.

I'd smelt it on him as he stood in the roadhouse, thinking he was God's gift, same as I can smell it on him now as he paces beside his shitty car half a kilometre away. The whiff of arrogance has waned, replaced by a nervous energy which bounces through the air up to Maxie and me.

Maxie ambles into action, the breeze ruffling his mane, deciding to pick his way down the slope a second before I do. When a good horse acts on your thoughts, it's uncanny. When Maxie does it, it makes my scalp prickle.

The man with the black curls is too busy thumping his hands on the car roof and pleading with his phone to notice us. He startles when I call out, "Need a hand there?"

"Oh thank God," he says, relief easing the tension from his face. He squints up at me. "My car, the engine light came on, all these other lights too. I had to pull over."

"You didn't exactly pick the best spot for it, did you?" I slide down from Maxie and nod at the Commodore. "I'll have a look for you, see if I can figure out what's happened."

"Great, great," he blurts. "Me name's Leon, by the way."

He stares at me as though that should mean something, but I don't know any Leons so I just shrug. "Okay."

The sweat beading on his face spoils the veneer of his grin. "I looked but . . . you know." He shrugs, his gaze sliding down to my arse as I pop the bonnet and prop it open. "D'ya know a bit about cars?"

"I hope so." I'm not about to tell him I'm a mechanic now. The air clinging to this bloke is greasier than a sump gasket. I lean over the engine bay to peer at the coolant reservoir. The radiator is hot, but the car has sat here long enough to stop the coolant boiling out. I leave the cap open half a twist to keep cooling while I check everything else.

Leon's feet scuff the gravel behind me, followed by the crunch of Maxie's hooves as he steps between me and the man. The horse pins his ears back and raises his head.

"Nice horse," Leon says, but Maxie isn't. He was a bloody ratbag when he was alive, and he still is now. Leon might know a bit about the native animals he's come here to steal, but I don't reckon he knows enough about horses to notice the slightly jerky way Maxie's legs bend and straighten, or the not-quite-right way his grey coat catches the sun. Let alone how his eyes are as flat and shiny as a taxidermied animal, not liquid amber like a real horse's.

Leon at least senses the wisdom of moving away from Maxie, and from me. He shuffles into view on my left-hand side. "Whaddaya reckon?" A tremor pitches through his voice.

Instead of telling him I reckon he stole a very shitty car, I say, "You should've had it serviced before you left Sydney. There's bugger-all coolant in the radiator. You're lucky you stopped before cooking it." I straighten, flicking my pony-tail back over my shoulder. "You got some coolant? It needs topping up before you can go anywhere."

He glances at his watch. "Shit. Shit." Glances at me. "Coolant? I dunno. I'll have a look, hey." He dives into the back seat, rummaging. Red dirt stains his shoes and ankles. Fingers of dust stretch up his calves.

"What about in the boot?" I ask.

"No." He jerks up, hitting his head on the roof as he backs out of the car. "Not in the boot." Maybe he has empty crates in there too, for this consignment of reptiles.

Leon swipes the back of one hand across his lips. He flexes the other hand then forms a fist, over and over. What would he do to me if he knew I knew his dirty little secret?

He says, "How far is Dry Creek from here?"

"Two clicks, but you'll blow your engine if you don't sort out that radiator first. We'll have to use your water bottle, if you didn't bring coolant or anything else with you." I shrug. "It's not the best for these cars but it'll be enough to get you back to town. You want to be putting a fifty-fifty mix into these models, keep the coolant right up to 'em because they're thirsty on it."

He retrieves a drink bottle from the car, hands it to me. "I was saving it until I could get help, you know, like they say." He plucks the front of his t-shirt away from his skin. It sticks to the damp patches under his armpits. "How d'ya stand it out here? It's not right, all this silence."

I twist my mouth into a grin. "The quiet is exactly why I'm here. It was too busy for me in the city. Too many people making too much noise." At first, it was all a swell of excitement, like standing in a mosh pit anticipating the band coming on to start playing, then the exhilaration when they did. "I feel too much, though and there's too much to feel in a place where people live jammed in on top of each other."

Their emotions still sit with me, even after all these years, queasy on my conscience. Standing on wet sand with the Pacific Ocean washing my feet and the city's pain needling my skin. Broken hearts on the breeze, the taste of tears on my lips. It got so I could tell which feeling came from who, and why. The bitter-almond shame from a businesswoman who screwed her intern while her husband struggled at home to cook dinner, make lunches and get the kids washed and into bed. The copper heartache of doomed teenage first love. Green jelly gambling, red if it was someone else's money.

No matter where I went, the noise didn't let up until I fled to these big skies out west and found Kody.

Squeezing my eyes shut, I bring myself back to the present, with the warmth of a broken-down car under my palms, a not-horse standing behind me, and the weight of the curly-haired man's expectations.

I tip all Leon's water into the radiator. He swallows, checking his watch again.

"Meeting someone, eh?" My question hangs in the thick air for a heartbeat, then falls flat.

"That was the only water I brought." He takes the empty bottle off me, peers into it. Judging by the copper scent coming off him, he's not going to live long enough for dehydration to be a problem.

The scent creeps over the back of my tongue into my throat before I can turn away. Nausea washes through my belly. "We found these stones on our property, hey, in a creek bed, like they were ready to be discovered." I say, unsure why I'm confiding in him. Maybe I'm hoping it will make me feel better about what's about to happen, because dead men can't tell secrets. "Two big smooth stones, perfect for skimming in the river, and as blue as the Bay of Fires."

Leon stares at me, maybe wondering if I'm unhinged. A muscle tics under his left eye. "Were they opals?"

So, he's not completely stupid then, even though no-one's ever found opals in our area. "Sort of, but they're not. You can't cut them, or even chip them." Grinning, I lean towards him. "You won't believe me, but one of those stones is in this horse, right about where his heart should be."

Leon bunches one hand into a fist. He's palmed a rock, doesn't bother hiding it. My heart beats a little faster. Does he reckon he might kill me with it?

"Is the coolant okay now?"

"There's enough in the radiator to get you where you need to go." I screw the cap back on. "Start her up, hey."

The rock thuds onto the ground. Leon scrambles around the open car door into the driver's seat, slamming the door shut. It only takes a second for the engine to kick over.

Maxie waits behind me until I drop the bonnet. Leon might've run me down otherwise, but he must realise that hitting half a ton of horse won't end well. Especially not a horse sculpted out of metal.

Stones flick up from the Commodore's rear wheels as Leon reverses away. The car skids in a messy arc, engine revving and rear wheels spinning before it disappears down the road.

I don't reckon Leon had a clue what sort of place he was coming to when he agreed to smuggle wildlife out of here. On second thoughts, he *can't* have known. No-one does, not even me.

* * *

Maxie stands with one hindleg cocked, unfazed by the car peeling away from us. I lay my hand on his shoulder, tracing

97

the shape of hard steel under his soft coat. A real horse would have muscle fibres all running in one direction then splicing where one muscle sits beside the next, not high tensile cable like Maxie.

My backside hardly hits the saddle before he takes off. I find my other stirrup, balancing into his big stride. Although I'm too stubborn to admit I'm not quite reconciled with riding Kody's creation, the big steel horse does have his advantages. He doesn't sweat or shit or eat, doesn't get tired or bored or sick. Whatever bits of the real Maxie remain are enough to make him behave like a real horse most of the time.

Which makes him pretty bloody unpredictable.

I don't know if it's the horse part of him or the other that means I'm just a passenger right now, not the one in charge. Most of the time I'd rather ride one of my flesh and blood horses, but on a day like today Maxie is better suited to the job.

He plows up the slope, his impenetrable legs thrashing through the saltbush. Wildflowers still peep through in places, a legacy from the good spring we've just had, when colour carpeted the red dirt. It's no wonder the brushmen of the bush loved the western region so much, where light and colour play in an ever-changing ebb and flow. The outback hues take my breath away and make my heart sing all at once.

Maxie shifts and flows around rocks and ruts in the ground with the slightest touch on his reins, or a shifting of my seat or a squeeze of my legs. Early on, he'd had no sense of self-preservation so our first few rides involved charging straight into the middle of old man saltbushes, stumbling into ditches, or me getting scraped off by tree branches.

I'd almost given up on Maxie when an inkling of real horse emerged from him—an understanding of how to avoid obstacles like any live horse did, of not clanging his steel bones against any rocks or stumps he walked past. It was a revelation. My steel horse could learn.

We still weren't sure what to make of Maxie's second coming. No-one planned for it to happen, because Kody had only ever intended to sculpt a horse to display at our house gate. One night, as he'd gotten closer to finishing his new piece, he chucked an old saddle blanket over the sculpture's loins to sit his tools on, then left it there overnight.

The blanket was still covered in grey hair even though old Maxie had been dead since last winter. Grey horse hair is hard as hell to get rid of, and so we'd often find a strand or two clinging to our clothes whenever we came out of the shed, to remind us of the big fella.

Heat had wrapped the land without letting go that evening, so Kody and me sat out on the back verandah nursing stubbies and watching a blue aurora paint the sky. In the morning, the sculpture stood in the shed right where Kody had left it, still with the saddle blanket across its loins, but skin and sleek grey hair covered those metal bones—the same grey as the hair on the saddle blanket, with a mane and tail to boot.

At the sound of our footsteps, the horse that wasn't a horse turned its head towards us, ears pricked. It whinnied. Kody couldn't hear it, of course, but it was the perfect replica of a real horse, and the sight alone of it moving was enough to send the two of us bolting outside to scramble back into the ute.

"How did you do that?" I'd grabbed Kody's sleeve. We peered past the crack bisecting the grimy windscreen from roof to bonnet.

"I set the smaller stone in his chest," Kody said, his hands shaking around the words. "Used that saddle blanket to rest on, all covered in Maxie's hair."

We didn't know what else to do, so we cowered on the bench seat, unable to look away from the shed door. After a long while, the horse that wasn't wobbled out into the yard. The saddle blanket slipped off its rump into the dirt. It saw the herd in the house paddock and headed over, neighing. That sent my horses wild, of course, even though Kody's sculptures weren't new to them. But one that looked like a horse, sounded like a horse? No way.

Eventually they stopped bolting around the paddock for long enough to edge closer, with plenty more snorting and spooking, to meet the sculpture waiting at the fence with its ears pricked towards the herd. After that, it didn't take long for them start grazing again. The horse that wasn't didn't graze—didn't need to, of course—but it did cock a hindleg and lower its head with ears relaxed and at ease.

It took me and Kody much longer to come to grips with the fact a sculpture, a stone found by chance in a creek bed, and a saddle blanket had somehow melded into a sort-of robot that thought it was a horse. Right from the start though, we swore never to tell another living soul about it.

* * *

It takes me the same amount of time to cut across the hills as it does for Leon to speed his white Commodore around to Dry Creek crossing. I pull Maxie up just over the crest of the hill and look down into the valley. Even though I'd had my suspicions about who'd be out here, the sight of the Hilux parked under a tree still hits me hard in the guts. Nausea seeps through me as I sit taller in the saddle, steeling myself for what's about to come.

Before Leon reaches the crossing, the Commodore thuds out one final protest from under the bonnet as it shits itself. He steers it into a sliding stop on the shoulder then jumps out into a cloud of smoke, clutching his forehead. I bet he's cursing me, even though he'd already stuffed the engine before I found him.

The Hilux pulls out onto the road to cruise the few hundred metres up to Leon. Sunlight catches the chrome around its front grille. I bite my lip as Shayna Durlow gets out of her flash new truck. Her ponytail swings and bounces as she approaches Leon. For a second I wonder if they're lovers, but she only shakes his hand from a polite distance.

Anyway, I don't reckon Leon's been out here before, and the one who came last time was a woman in her forties. No-one found her, either. Only her car abandoned beside the highway twenty kilometres south of town. If the gossip about that had made Shayna nervous, it wasn't enough to stop her being here today.

Turning my head, I strain to hear what Leon is saying to Shayna. I'm too far away and his words are lost on the breeze. He must be talking about his car because she glances in the direction he's come from, maybe wondering if whoever helped him is still out here. A muscle twitches under my breastbone. It was stupid telling Leon about the stones, even if he isn't going to live long enough to blab to anyone except Shayna. With any luck my horse is the last animal either of them is interested in talking about.

Maxie shifts into a steady walk down the hill. "Oh shit, no." I pick up my reins but I may as well be trying to convince a freight train to stop. If I jump off he might hoof it, leaving me stuck more than sixty kilometres from home. All I can do is stay put and see what happens next.

Leon retrieves a sports bag from the boot and unzips it on the bonnet of his car. Shayna leans close to see what's inside. Money to buy whatever animals are caged in her ute, I reckon. Leon staggers back from the bag, clapping his hands to his cheeks. Shouting, Shayna grabs him by a fistful of tank-top. He gabbles, waving his hands up and down.

Anger and fear vibrate the air like a tuning fork, a scattering of emotion which forces me to cringe and curl away. Maxie's stride is forceful, determined, a beat to match the hammering of my heart.

Shayna shoves Leon away. She scoops her hand into the bag then flings it up, scattering a thousand grains of red dirt in the air between them.

"It wasn't me, I swear." He shrinks back, holding his palms out to her. By the time his feet stop moving, I'm close enough to see redness swirling around his legs. The dust stains his thighs, creeps higher to eclipse his shorts. His hands. Freezing him on the spot. His screams echo in my ears, even when I clap my palms flat over them.

Leon keeps screaming until the dust reaches his chin, fills his open mouth. It races up to consume his head.

My guts twist as I retch. Sand spills out of my mouth, harsh against my teeth, dry where it falls into the breeze. I try to fill my lungs without gasping, because for a crazy moment there's pressure on my chest, squashing the breath right out of me, too.

Shayna trips on a rock as she backpedals from Leon, landing on her arse. Dirt smears her jeans and shirt. The Leon-shaped sand sculpture crumbles, at first just a few red grains teasing free on the breeze. Then, like an invisible hand has pulled a loose thread, Leon scatters on the wind. Every bit of him becomes nothingness, even those once-white shoes.

Maxie leaps into a canter, still ignoring my attempts to turn him away from this mess. Hysterical laughter spills out of my mouth, mixing with a string of sand-tinged spit. Whatever is happening, I can't explain it. I just know I'm part of it, and fated to see it through to the end.

Shayna spots us heading towards her. Sobbing, she pushes herself to her feet and sprints for the Hilux.

Her brand new car doesn't start.

Maxie.

I flatten my palm on the horse's neck. The coolness grounds me, dulls the pepper of Shayna's panic, of Leon's fear which still hangs thick in the summer day. Part of Koby's soul is welded into every one of his artworks. Somehow, his calmness enhances this horse. The blue stone set in Maxie's steel ribcage is the same colour as my love's eyes.

The tang of oiled metal coats my tongue. Shayna Durlow won't beg for her life the way Leon begged her. The top of her head appears beside the ute, just enough to aim the .22 calibre rifle she's positioned on the bonnet.

Swearing, I throw myself sideways out of the saddle, clinging to the pommel with one hand. Maxie's hooves thud into the dirt a few feet away from my cheek. The gunshot shatters the air, blasting away any last traces of Leon. The bullet pings when it hits Maxie, rattles around inside for a moment. A piece of metal drops and clatters away in our wake. I hang there out of the saddle, anticipating that Shayna is reloading the rifle, steadying her next shot.

It never comes.

Maxie's big hooves trample the spot where Leon turned into dust. Shayna swings the rifle around to meet us, pulls the trigger. It clicks. A misfire. She drops it, hurls herself into the driver's seat of the Hilux. The ute's central locking bolts home, then unlocks, over and over.

One of Maxie's hooves lands on the rifle, crushing the barrel.

Shayna stares at me, her eyes huge in a face framed by dishevelled hair that's escaped from her ponytail. I jump down from Maxie. Striding towards the car, my own emotions flood my senses, for once. Anger sandblasts away any compassion I might've once summoned for this bitch. She hollers as I fling the door open, digging her bootheels into the footwell in an effort to push herself over the console, away from me.

A regurgitation of excuses pours out of her mouth. "Please. Please. I'm a mother, like you, Mia. A wife, like you."

"You're nothing like me," I snarl, my mouth twisting. Do her lies taste as acrid on her tongue as they do on mine?

She struggles when I catch her wrist, but she can't stop me from hauling her out onto the gravel. "I didn't hurt anyone," she says. Hair falls across her cheeks, blotting the snot-streaked tears there. "We need the money. We're going under. I told Chris I got an inheritance."

I slap her hand away from my sleeve. "He must've found that a coincidence then, considering all the cages of native animals you've been storing in your shed. Whatcha got in the back of your ute, hey, some shinglebacks? A few pythons? Are you poaching parrots for them, too?"

"No, no. You can't tell anyone. Please."

"How many of them die from the stress, Shayna? The fear? How many did you bring for Leon?" Rage flares inside me.

She launches at me, her flailing hands scratching my face, yanking my hair. I glimpse a blur behind her, then an almighty clang drives every other sound out of my head. Maxie closes his mouth on Shayna's shoulder, drags her off me, backs up a half-dozen steps and stands still with her dangling from his teeth, unfazed by her shrieks and threats.

I put one hand out to steady myself, then look up at Shayna.

As though she's guessed what I'm thinking, her eyes narrow. "Go on, kill me then."

I laugh. "I'm not going to kill you. You need to explain to your mate in Sydney why his couriers keep disappearing when they meet you. How's he going to take it when you tell him you don't have his animals or his money?"

Maxie doesn't spit Shayna out, just opens his mouth so she drops to the ground. She glares up at me, her chest heaving. "He's not my mate."

"He sure as shit won't be now." I shrug. "But he's your problem, not mine."

"I've got some money." She points to the Commodore. Red sand spills out of the bag on the car bonnet, trailing down the white paint before the breeze steals it away. There's no sight or scent of cash in the bag anymore.

Squatting in front of her, I scoop up a handful of dirt. "Don't forget, Shayna, in the end everything turns to dust."

"My car won't start."

I cock an eyebrow at her. Her hate tastes like poison inside my cheek. "I hope you know a good mechanic, then." Maxie moves to me when I touch his rein. I swing onto his back, only realising when my arse hits the saddle how much my legs are trembling.

"You can't just leave me here." Fear cracks through Shayna's belligerent tone.

"I reckon you'll need the time to work out how to explain this to the police, don't you?" I gesture from her car to Leon's. With any luck, my anonymous phone call from the booth near the milk bar means the police are already looking into how Shayna Durlow will be at Dry Creek crossing right now with a car full of wildlife she's trapped to sell for big money to some bastard smuggler.

The coppers already knew someone was trafficking, just not who. I don't stick around to watch them haul Shayna's arse into the station though. My family is waiting for me at home.

* * *

Maxie gets me back to our place in time to have lunch ready when Kody and Evie come in from the paddock. We spend the afternoon moving our main herd of cattle down to the flood plain, which is thick with feed. After dinner, I bathe Evie and tuck her into bed, drunk on the bliss of her little giggles. I lie with her until the tiny arms clenched around my neck relax with sleep. My heart swells, fierce with love for my family.

I settle out on the porch with a cuppa. Kody sprawls in the chair next to me, holding a mug in one hand and my hand in the other. Even in the moonless night I can sketch the shape of our horses grazing in their paddock. Maxie stands with them, his head turned and ears pricked. Watching. Waiting.

Above them, a palette of blue unfurls across the black sky, colours which dance and merge. Blue like my love's eyes. Blue like two stones once nestled in a creek bed.

About the Author:

Faran Silverton is a fantasy writer whose work is influenced by her experiences living and travelling in rural Australia. She currently lives on Kaurna land. Her stories explore animal behaviour and the human-animal bond, coming from over 30 years working in the animal industry. She graduated with an Advanced Diploma of Arts in Professional Writing from the Adelaide College for the Arts, South Australia, and has attended masterclasses with Bryce Courtenay and Fiona McIntosh.

Find her at www.faransilverton.com

The Snowy Mountains are the highest mountain
range in Australia, and the most dangerous.
You don't name a place 'Perisher' without reason ...

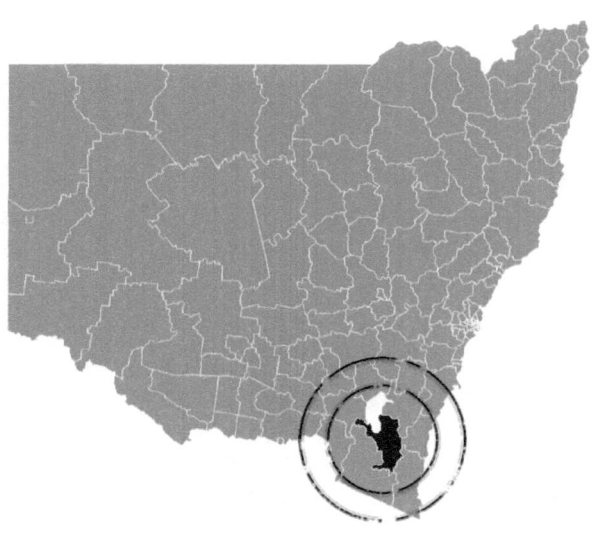

BRUMBIETHORN

M. R. Mortimer

I arrived in Cooma on the twenty first of June. My wife and son were with me, but I was working, they were just along for the ride. I'd been asked a favour by some old friends. The town was overflowing with visitors, more so than any ski season I could recall, we were only able to get our room at the Alpine Hotel because of a cancellation.

The Snowy Mountains had been the scene of a recent death. They weren't so snowy anymore, and the region was seeing unusual growth in visitors, as people fled the coast. There had been some . . . issues in the bigger cities, and the result was an exodus. The global temperatures had been steadily increasing over the last decade, and things were going pear shaped. You just had to watch the animals to know something was wrong.

My friends in America had three sons. Two of them—Trevor and Thomas—were visiting here. One had died in the mountains. The other wasn't making any sense to anybody. I was here to find out what happened.

My wife and son stayed at the Alpine Hotel, while I headed for my first appointment at the hospital on Bent Street. Jazz would find something to entertain Eli while I was gone. Trevor Polstaff was being held at the hospital under guard, suspected murderer of his brother Thomas. My appointment was a meeting with the hospital registrar overseeing Trevor's case.

Jenny Walsh met me under the concrete awning near the small car park at the front of the hospital. It was a small building, not like the big hospitals in the city, and I had to wonder how well equipped they were for the increased number of visitors, should anything bad happen.

I offered my hand to shake, but Jenny ignored it, turned, and led me inside.

"Mr Martin," she said. "We need to make this quick. It's a busy hospital right now, and distractions like yours are a luxury I can ill afford."

"Can I speak with Trevor, at least?"

"You can try, but he's not going to reply. You'd have more luck getting a straight answer out of his dead brother. Frankly you should leave and let the police do their jobs. But if you want to talk to them, this is the officer in charge of the case."

She handed me a business card with the NSW police logo on it. I stayed quiet as she led me through the hospital which was bustling like a small town facility never does.

"I know there are a lot of visitors in town, but why so many patients?" I asked.

"The snow season only just started, but it's just a feeble coat of powder, so that means more accidents, and greater damage done. Even experienced skiers are hurting themselves, because they aren't accommodating for the reduced coverage."

We had reached a door to a private ward, two police officers standing outside. They nodded to Jenny as we approached. She pushed open the door and waved me through. "This is Trevor. I advise you not to stay too long. I'll be able to answer a couple of questions, but I only have a few minutes."

The man on the bed was gaunt, tossing and turning in a slow, macabre horizontal dance, muttering. Every now and then a word passed his lips. "Creature," "horn," or "darkness" being repeated several times while I was there. As if in some strange dialogue, there were muffled noises from another room, similar to Trevor's mutterings.

"What happened to him?" I asked.

"He was in a hiking party of six. They found him alive and four dead. The last one, a woman, is still missing."

"And what of the four?"

"All dead. Impaled by something. The coroner will have more details, if you need them."

"And who's that, making the same noises?"

"That? That's the coroner's assistant. He handled the bodies, held the wounds open during the autopsy, and damaged a glove. The wounds were laced with a powerful neurotoxin. Not something we've seen before, but we believe the assistant is suffering from the same exposure as Trevor. Nobody knows where Trevor got the toxin or why he may have killed the rest of the hikers."

"You are that sure he did it?"

"It's the only answer we have for now. Unless the police uncover another suspect. My job is to treat him, not judge him. Any possible guilt will be assigned by the detectives."

"Guilty until they find the woman?"

"My guess is she's dead too, but that's also a matter for the police. Until a body is found or she comes here for treatment, I can't say anything about her situation. Now, if you'll excuse me, I have other duties."

"Of course," I replied. "Thank you for your time."

Trevor's muttering, moaning and grunts continued. It was clear I'd never get any answers from that poor soul, but I approached his bedside anyway. He looked through me with deep, troubled eyes.

"What happened to you?" I asked.

His muttering turned to shouting. "Creature! Horn! Darkness! Creature! Horn! Darkness!" he screamed, and a nurse came running in.

"I'm sorry Sir, but you will have to leave. He upsets the other patients when he's like this, and you are distressing him."

I took out my phone as I left the room and called Trevor's parents, as I had promised. It went to voicemail. I guessed the time difference meant they were asleep. I left a message.

"It's me. Yes, I saw him. He's alive, but I'm sorry, I'll say it straight—there's nothing of the Trevor you know. Yes, I'll keep looking. They don't seem to know much. There's another victim the same. It's a neurotoxin. I'll find out more and call again. Don't worry, I'll get you more answers."

I put the phone in my pocket and closed my eyes for a moment. I opened them to a crazed face; a man in his sixties, broad grin and wide eyes, about three inches from my nose. His sun-dried skin was that of a man of the land. He had mischief in his gap-toothed smile.

"I know what happened to the boy," he hissed. "None of this lot will listen to me though. But I know what did it. I know what killed the other ones, too."

"So it wasn't him?"

"Ha! No. That boy didn't do it. But I can show you what did. You interested?"

"Who are you?"

"Name's Bill Murphy. Mad Bill Murphy they call me 'round here."

"Roy," I replied. "Roy Martin. How is it you know what happened?"

"I live up the mountain. I know what it was. I've been tracking it for a long time. The cops were chattering about this on the scanner, so I came down to see if I could get heard. I knew as soon as they said that one was mad and the others stabbed with a thick something, like a branch. It's the madness gives it away."

"You said what, not who did it . . ." I said, stepping around him to walk down the corridor, the two police officers chuckling at some joke.

"They wasn't no who, that's why." He followed me, casting the police officers a scowl.

"Then what? What did this?"

"A brumbiethorn. It did the stabbing, and the maddening."

"What the hell is a brumbiethorn?" I said, stopping to look at him.

"Come on, we have time. I'll take you up the mountain, you'll be back to your hotel by dinner." Now it was his turn to walk ahead, as he made for the exit.

"Oh, the hotel. I left my wife and son there . . ." I rushed after him.

"Best fetch them. If the brumbiethorns are coming down the mountain, you'll be better off together than apart."

"What the hell is a brumbiethorn?" I asked again, louder this time, feeling many eyes on me in the crowded lobby.

"It'll be easier to show you." He left the building, not waiting for me.

I followed him out to the car park. He walked to a beat-up old ute, while I jumped in my SUV.

"Get your family, then I'll lead the way," he yelled.

I'm still not sure why I thought dragging them to a strange place with this weird old man was a good idea, but I took out my phone and rang Jazz. She said they were at the bakery next door to the hotel. I rushed around and collected them.

"What's going on?" Jazz asked as she climbed in, glancing with distrust at the old man in the ute that pulled up along side, blocking traffic.

"This is Bill," I replied as Eli buckled himself into the child seat in the back. "He knows about what happened to the boys. He's got something to show us up the mountain."

"With all due respect to Bill," Jazz said, nodding at the old man through the lowered windows of our vehicles. "Taking our son somewhere up the mountain with a strange old man we don't know seems a bit irresponsible."

"Even if there is something bigger going on, something more dangerous than just five hikers getting killed and another going nuts?" I replied.

"How big?"

117

"Real big!" Bill said. "That one lost his marbles, they got another bloke who lost it just from handling the bodies. Oh and yeah, bodies. They found five so far. One hiker missing, who knows if the creatures have got anybody else?"

"Creatures?" The distrust was clear in Jazz's tone. "What creatures?"

"That's what I'm going to show you. The clowns down here don't want to believe it, but I can show you the proof. Besides, it's a nice drive into the mountains, you'll be back for dinner, and if you think I'm dangerous, ask a local."

"Hey," Jazz called out, with no hesitation, to a passing woman. "Is this guy in the ute dangerous?"

"Mad Bill Murphy?" the woman said. "No, he's harmless. Mad as a cut snake, but harmless. Just don't go falling for his crazy stories."

"Ya see?" Bill said. "Harmless. You'll be safe if you stick close to me, but these others got no idea what's coming."

"Fine," Jazz said. "Let's get this over with."

We followed Bill for nearly an hour, until we drove through the village at Braemar Bay. He pulled into the driveway of an old farm house to the west of the town, and we followed. As we piled out of the car, Bill waved us around to a shed and ushered us inside.

"It's here somewhere, just a minute." He swept a bunch of old cans and tools to the side of a weathered workbench, then rummaged through a cupboard.

After a few minutes, with us inspecting our surroundings in a nervous agitation, worrying about the kind of things anybody who's seen Wolf's Creek might, he grunted and lifted something wrapped in cloth, and carried it to the bench.

"This is what it was killed them hikers," he said, as he removed the cloth. "The old man gave me this when he told me the stories."

It was a skull, a large one at that. By the shape, I would have said it belonged to a horse, except for the massive horn protruding from the forehead. The horn was thick, and around two and a half times the length of the skull itself. I reached to touch it as Jazz held Eli close, her expression one of concern for our safety.

"Don't touch it!" Bill shouted. "It's fragile now. But when it was still fresh, or the creature was alive, that horn had a secretion which coats it. It's a powerful poison, will send you mad, like that poor lad in the hospital. I couldn't tell you how long it's effects last when it's dry."

Bill picked up the skull and brought it closer.

"I can touch it because I've spent the last fifty years building up an immunity."

"I find that hard to believe," Jazz muttered.

"What is it?" Eli asked, wide eyed and curious.

"It's a skull, boy!" Bill snapped. "Haven't you seen a skull before?"

"What's it from?" Jazz asked, holding Eli tighter than before.

"A brumbiethorn."

"A what?" Jazz asked.

"A brumbiethorn. It had a traditional name, before the settlers came, but I don't know, that's one of those secrets of traditional knowledge lost to time. The old man, that's what we called him, he wasn't my father though, he was my step-grandfather, he told me about them."

"So it's like a horse, with a horn?" I asked.

"It's a unicorn kind of thing, yes. But it's not one of your fairy-tale things of glitter and rainbows, son. This one is dangerous. Beautiful, majestic, and deadly. It'll kill you faster than you can whip out your phone for help."

"Are they aggressive?" Jazz asked.

"They tend to be reclusive, and avoid being seen. I've never seen a live one, just this skull. But there is a story, a kind of prophecy the old man told me as a boy. He said that when the people fail in their duty to look after this land, then the brumbiethorns will come down the mountain, and retribution will be taken."

"A creature like this," I said. "It'd be top of the food chain I guess."

"Not exactly," Bill said. "They eat grass, not animals, but they're territorial. Though they have their enemies in the mountains."

"What would hunt something like that?" Jazz asked.

"Drop bears are their greatest threat. The bastards drop on the neck of the brumbiethorn, so they can't defend themselves with the horn. Then they swarm it. They eat everything but the skull, and a few bones."

"Drop bears are make believe!" Eli snapped with all the confidence of his ten years.

"So is Santa Claus!" Bill growled. "What's your point, boy?"

Eli cowered behind Jazz, looking up at her in confusion.

Bill covered the skull, then continued. "Up on these mountains, everything is real. It's that kind of place. Imagination, storytelling, reality, it all blurs. There is no such thing as fiction on this land. Especially when the fog rolls in."

"So you are telling us there is a brumbiethorn, out there, killing people?" I asked.

"Not just one," Bill said. "If they're getting ready to come down the mountain, like the story says, there may be hundreds, perhaps thousands, up there in the fog."

Bill walked to the door, waving us through. The old man closed the shed and locked it, then leaned on it, almost nonchalant. "I know where that hiking party was attacked, if you want me to show you. It's another half hour up, if you want to go. Or we can have a coffee and talk in the house. Up to you."

"I wouldn't mind a coffee, but I came here for answers. I'd like to see that place."

"We'll take your car then," Bill said, walking towards it. "It should be able to make the track."

We got in, Jazz in the back with Eli, Bill in the front, and I drove. He leaned forward, pointing directions. One question nagged at me.

"Where did they come from? The brumbiethorns? I mean, horses only came with the first fleet, right?"

"They aren't horses, son." Bill replied. "The old man told me they were here before the first people. They been here tens of thousands of years, maybe came over that land bridge thing way back when. Or maybe they were already here. Maybe those unicorns in Europe were from here to start with. I dunno, but they're ancient."

Jazz reached forward, her seatbelt off, and turned up the radio. We took the hint. Bill continued pointing the way, and the road became a track, then was barely even that, but the trusty SUV took it all. After around forty minutes of this, we entered a clearing. It was a well-used camp site, but nobody was there. A dark shape lurked in the trees opposite, and then moved, into the open. Bill fumbled with his seatbelt buckle in his excitement, determined to get out of the car for a closer look.

"I've searched my whole life for you, you beautiful creature," he mumbled as he opened the door, then demanded, "Get your phone out, start filming! We might never see it again! And for God's sake, stay in the car!"

Bill slammed the door and walked across the open clearing. Jazz, leaning between the front seats, got it all on her phone's camera. The creature stepped forward and looked up, straight at the mad fool. Its body, shiny black, glistened in the late afternoon sun speckled through the trees. The horn, majestic and deadly, rose from its head into the light. The horn was stained a dull brown from the dried blood of its victims, yet wet looking, from the coating of venom.

The thing was huge, bigger than a regular horse, though not as big as a good draft horse. I never got the hang of the measurement in hands, but this thing, this was big. It snorted, stamped its feet, and lowered its head. Bill stopped, turned, and ran. Jazz, stricken with terror, never stopped filming. Another, then a third brumbiethorn entered the clearing. Then came a fourth, a fifth, in many varied colours, but all as terrifying as each other.

123

Running towards us, Bill screamed, his eyes wide in sheer terror. A moment later, the horn of the first beast erupted from his chest as he was lifted off the ground, then tossed to the side. There was no hope for him. Slamming the car into reverse, I floored the accelerator and turned the wheel, churning the ground as the tyres spun. The engine roared as I thumped it into drive and headed out of the clearing. The beast smashed hard against the side of the car, making a guttural noise from my nightmares.

Jazz never dropped the phone. We sped down the trail with the creature behind us, catching flashes of more of them, in the dappled light between the trees. A glance in the review mirrors showed destruction. The mob stormed down the mountain, flattening everything in their path.

Even once we reached the open road, they followed close behind. I didn't lose sight of the creatures until we were passing Bill's house.

We flew through Braemar Bay at high speed leaning on the horn and shouting out the windows.

"Run or get inside! Brumbiethorns! Get to safety!"

We didn't wait to see if anybody heeded our words. We had lost site of the creatures, but I wasn't about to stop. I rummaged in my pocket for the card the hospital registrar had given me, and passed it to Jazz.

"Send the police the video, tell them this is what killed the hikers, that Trevor is innocent."

"On it," she said, taking the card in shaking hands. "I've already sent it to the news channels. Everybody's got to get off the mountain. Those things are indiscriminant. They'll kill everything."

Scenery flashed by, and I ignored it, racing down the mountains as fast as possible. There was nothing else for it, we had to get out of the area. There was no way of knowing how far those things would follow, but I was heading home. At least we had some warning, and I could strengthen the fences in preparation. And Trevor and Thomas' parent's, how could I tell them? They'd see the video on the TV news before I could stop and call them.

We flew through Cooma without stopping. I couldn't have gotten Trevor out of the hospital, not while he will still suffering the effects of the venom. He'd be safer behind those walls than with us. The radio station crackled, so I turned the radio to the local ABC station.

". . . which have stormed through Braemar Bay," the presenter was saying. "They are heading towards Cooma. These things are dangerous, we urge our listeners to stay indoors. We'll keep you informed as news comes to hand. An eyewitness caller, as you just heard, called them Brumbiethorns, as did the vehicle which flew through town

125

moments before the herd. Their warning saved our caller's life, but she hasn't yet found her three children, and our hearts go out to all the families wondering about loved ones in this developing situation. Several eyewitnesses in Braemar Bay have sent in videos, you can find those on our website."

There was silence for a moment, just the engine and the crackle of the radio as we passed under high tension power lines, before the radio presenter continued.

"Beware the brumbiethorn."

About the Author:

M R Mortimer is a NSW based SFF writer, former teacher and anthropologist, currently living and working on Wiradjuri land.

His available works include his Fantasy trilogy The Cinder Chronicles, several stand alone Science Fiction novels, and a short story collection. More information can be found on his website at suspendedearth.com.

The Royal National Park, just south of Sydney, is characterised by secluded beaches, cliffs and eucalyptus rich bushland. Covering over 150 square kilometres, this park is home to more than just kookaburras, lyre birds and echidnas.

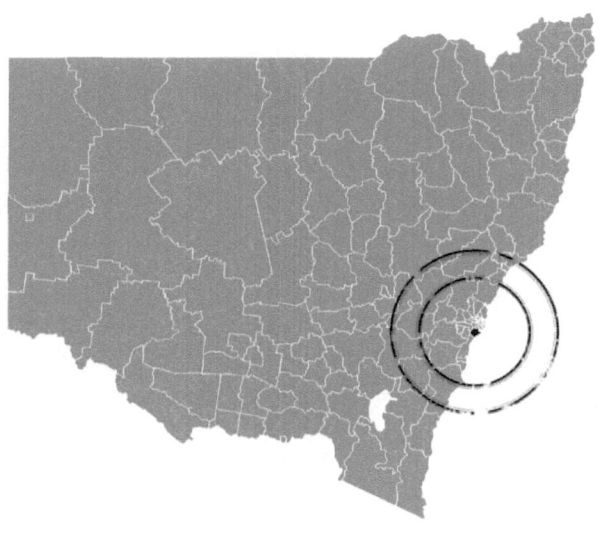

LITTLE RED

Lucy Fox

It's Easter lunch. Your extended family gather around the
trestle-tables, opinions spilling from their lips. That's our
catalyst, of sorts. But your story began long before you sat
down on the fold-out chair next to your younger cousin, Amy.
It started back in high school, when your P.E. teacher—with the
fluffy blonde hair who exclusively wore tight-fitting velour
tracksuits—started to talk about sex. A nervous hush engulfed
your classroom. She informed you about the neighbouring
boys school, how you girls would soon fawn over them, how
this was natural, to proceed with caution. The giggles grew
louder, but you weren't laughing. You had no interest in talking
to boys—and to say they were attractive? That was absurd. You
knew you were misplaced but knew better than to bring it up.
Constantly Googling "how to tell if you're a lesbian?" despite
knowing you felt the same about girls as you did boys. You
laughed along when people said how amazing Channing
Tatum was, and pretended your love for Chris Hemsworth
wasn't due to him starring in a Marvel film.

You realised the profound awkwardness at watching sex scenes wasn't to do with your parents on the nearby couch. Most of the time, you could ignore it. But the disconnect would pop up every time a sexy woman beckoned you into the advertisement, every time a friend would boast about having sex, every time someone called you a virgin.

Amy whispers something that makes you almost drop the special Easter chicken (nine dollars from Coles) and tongs into the gravy boat.

"I've done it, Red. The V card is gone."

She's excited. You're uncertain how to respond. You don't get why it's news, or why she's telling you, but nod anyway, even throwing in an "Oh! Wow!" for decoration.

"You're next. You're the last one. The only one here who is still a"—she drops her voice an octave—"virgin."

Your face goes red—the reason for your nickname. Glancing around the table, everyone is in deep conversation. Your mother is talking to her brother, Tom. They resemble chattering birds. Your grandad is nodding along to whatever your brother Chris is saying. Your father is also part of that conversation but looks as though he'd rather be anywhere else. Grace, your sister, and your youngest cousin, Cherry, are in deep discussion about mountain goats. Aunty Millie isn't talking to anyone. She's staring directly at you. It always seems like her life goal is to make your life difficult. Your face burns.

"Aw, little Red," Aunty Millie calls across the table, directing everyone's eyes towards you. "What did Amy say?"

You look to Amy, hoping she'll throw you a bone.

"I was just telling her I lost my virginity," she says.

"Oh!" Grace chirps. "Congratulations! It's about bloody time!"

"Thanks!" Amy smiles in that vaguely condescending way. "Red's only red, because I asked her when she's planning on losing hers."

You want to vomit.

"We're thinking she's a lost cause. She's nearly twenty-three and virgining all over the place," your mother says.

"Come on Mum," Chris, says with a snort. "She's the youngest of the three of us. It's not her fault we set the precedent for losing it at fifteen!"

The whole table erupts into hearty laughter.

Your face is approximately two degrees hotter than the sun. "There's nothing wrong with being a virgin. Jesus' mum was a virgin, and aren't we here celebrating Jesus today?"

Your family may as well have been replaced by a pack of hyenas, they're cackling so loud.

Feeling your life expectancy dropping exponentially, it's almost a relief when the younger-and-no-longer-virginal Amy says, "Wait . . . are you a lesbian, Red?"

When you don't answer immediately, Chris assures you there's nothing wrong with being a lesbian. He has friends who are lesbians. You're almost comforted until he says: "But those girls are at it like rabbits. Such stamina. You'll be able to lose it that way, too, Red. No biggie."

"I'm a virgin. I don't care about sex. It's not the end of the fucking world!" You shovel peas and chicken into your mouth before you say anything else, and Grandad somehow diverts the conversation to plastic bags. He gives you the trademark wink he saves, special, for when he helps you out.

When the hubbub of chatter reignites, Amy whispers, "It'll happen for you one of these days," her voice still tinged with the superior flavour of an "experienced woman."

"If it does, I'll make sure not to tell you." The words come out more bitter than intended. You don't apologise.

"Prude," Amy mutters, but you hear it. It stings.

As soon as Grace starts collecting empty plates, you slip past everyone in the dining room, cross the hallway, and shut yourself in your bedroom. The carpet itches your feet. Running a hand along the bedside table and grabbing your phone, you take a seat on the bed. You want to scream or cry or die, but it's too hard to choose which.

As usual, Google's recommendation to fix an inactive sex drive involves eating a balanced diet, taking antidepressants, and masturbation.

It doesn't have any suggestions for how to make your family get off your back about something that doesn't impact them. Google can't explain how to be okay with the way you are—it can't even explain the way you are without trying to force medical treatments down your throat. You're tired of stressing over that Mayo Clinic article which labelled you with Hypoactive Sexual Desire Disorder.

Someone knocks at the door, and you hope it's Amy. Maybe coming to apologise for the public humiliation. Or wanting an apology for snapping at her. You want it to be Amy from months ago, virginity intact. Amy who used to stay up late with you and deconstruct romantic comedy tropes. Amy who didn't think having sex entitled her to a superiority complex. Amy who cared and didn't make you feel alone.

The door opens. It isn't Amy. It's Grandad. He leans against the doorframe. He's in the same checkered suit-vest and trousers he always wears—you and your cousins used to think he was like a cartoon character, with one outfit only.

"Alright, Red?" Your name always sounds safest on his tongue.

"Can you tell me another story, Grandad?" You scoot over on the bed to make space for him. "The last one about Vasilisa and Baba-Yaga got me through this week."

He straightens his back and smiles. "You're the only one who still cares for my stories."

133

You shrug. "You tell them like they're real."

Shutting the door, he sits on the bed. Even sitting, he's tall. His moustache is in line with your eyebrows. "Red, I think it's time you heard about the old Bundeena Quest."

You squint up at him. "A quest?"

"When I was young, there used to be a grand tradition. Every kid from Cronulla knew about it," he says. "On your eighteenth birthday, your friends would come together. As a group, you'd cross the river and head to Bundeena. The stories started before the ferry, back when you had to paddle across Port Hacking in dinghies, but it took on a life of its own once you could board the Curranulla. Once you'd get there, you'd find the special entrance and hike into the national park. There was a magical track to follow, and at the end, you'd find a little house."

"Was it a witch's house?"

"It was the house of Grandmother Love."

You roll your eyes and he taps you on the nose with a finger, like he did when you were a child.

"She'd tell your future. If you were to marry or divorce. She predicted your grandmother and I would meet in a supermarket. She knew we'd have a marvellous life, with two annoying children, and love each other until the end . . . Grandmother Love never was wrong . . ." He pauses a moment for reflection. "Back then, over sixty years ago,

Grandmother Love knew my brother would end up with his husband. Their relationship was illegal for decades, yet she knew they'd be happy together."

How wonderful, you think, to love one person for your whole life. How wonderful to never be alone because you're different.

"The Bundeena Quest died out years ago—they built a road into Bundeena, and the mystery vanished. Your parents' generation don't believe in anything magical . . . But I know you do, Red."

"You think I should go on this quest?"

"If you try, if you believe, if you trust, you will find the answer. Magic is everywhere, if you know where to look . . . But don't go alone—it's dangerous. Take Amy."

You think about Amy's smug expression over lunch and about finding out who you truly are. You think you have nothing to lose.

"I'm gonna go."

"My little Red," he says. "It's time you found a little bit of magic."

* * *

Nodding thanks to the crew member at the exit, you step over the gap between ferry and port. Following the crowd of towel-holding tourists up to the concrete walkway, you glimpse the street sign Grandad mentioned, and turn left down the empty stretch of road.

You walk at a considerable pace, mesmerised by the glamourous houses, and the snapshots of luminescent water between rooftops. You soon reach the end of the street, where a sign points to Jibbon beach, and half-climb half stumble down the sandy embankment to get to it.

The national park entrance is marked by two grand and blackened eucalypts, resembling what Grandad explained. As instructed, you pull a box of matches from your pocket and light one, placing it in the space between the trees. The sandy ground is littered with dozens of singed matches.

When the fire goes out, you say, "Woman of the woods. Godmother. Grandmother Love. Guide my feet to the future I seek. Bring me to your cottage door." You strike a second match, lay it between the trees. The flame goes out and you take a deep breath.

You cross the threshold.

Twigs crunch helplessly beneath your feet as you follow the leafy path. Nothing is a match for your Doc Martens, but prickly ferns snarl and scratch at your bare legs. The sun slips further behind the branches with each step. Tree trunks change from eucalypt grey to a darker brown. Ferns become more shrub-like, with deep, peculiar shades of green . . . fairy tale green. You try to ignore it, keeping your feet steady on the path—but was it normal for leaf-litter to turn into a trail of blooming April violets?

You slide over a mossy rock and steady yourself by the trunk of a pine tree. Perhaps the lush scenery was enough to fuel Grandad's wild imagination. Magic isn't real, you scoff while dense green shrubs emerge with every step, forcing you to stay on the path. Grandad is an old romantic.

You stop. A few metres ahead, the shrubbery quivers. You know it isn't a gust of wind as much as you want it to be.

Branches snap inside the bush. Your heart is a drumroll.

A furry snout pushes its way out of the glossy leaves. The nostrils flare in your direction. An enormous, clawed paw follows, and another. The creature emerges from the bush, and soon you stand face to face with a large, yellow-eyed wolf.

"Fuck."

The famous last word that would make any parent proud.

"Language." The wolf has a deep male voice.

You all but faint from shock. "Y-y-you can speak?"

"Y–y-yes I can." The wolf bares its teeth or smiles—it's hard to tell.

"I'm having a mid-life crisis at twenty-two," you say, running a hand through your hair.

"What brings you here?"

It's not wise to engage a wolf in conversation, but, of course, you do anyway. The wolf nods the whole way through your entire awkward and embarrassing life story. When you finish, it stands on its hind legs. "I can look like any man you desire."

You blink. "I just said I don't desire anyone."

"You mentioned Channing Tatum."

"Yeah, but—ugh!"

The wolf convulses. A dozen golf-ball-sized lumps sprout underneath its fur, making a squelching noise as they move under its skin. The wolf howls in agony. Eyes shut tight, you clench your teeth at the dreadful sound.

"Little Red, I'm everything you've been searching for." A heavy American accent coerces your eyes open.

Your jaw hangs open when you glance at the creature—no, at Channing Tatum.

"I can help," says the wolf in Channing's skin.

You're reminded of your teenage obsession. He's more handsome than you gave him credit for. Maybe you are straight and have simply lacked opportunity. You're aware of the heat in your cheeks, of him closing in. Your heart threatens to break your ribs.

The wolf-man grabs your hand and places it on his chest. "Come on, you're straight. You're just repressed. Let me help. Lose your virginity. Get your family off your back."

"I . . ."

138

He puts his hand on your waist. Tongue thick in your mouth, you're rooted to the spot. "Won't it feel so good to know for sure?" The Channing-wolf's eyes glow yellow.

"No," you say, stepping back. "I don't want to."

"What?"

"I don't want to have sex with you." It's a struggle to get the words out. "It doesn't matter who you look like. I can't—no, I don't want to."

"Fucking pricktease!" the creature shouts in a warped voice.

Breath catching in your chest, you back into a tree that wasn't there a moment ago.

The man's skin sprouts black fur in his anger. He keels over onto his hands and knees, turning back into the animal he is. "You filthy fucking lesbian."

You're frozen in panic. "I— I—"

The wolf bounds toward you. His heavy paws hit your chest. Your back scrapes hard against the tree bark. You can't breathe. "Take this as a warning." His snout is inches away, his breath hot and putrid. Claws sink into your skin.

You remember cutting off your fingertip with the kitchen knife. You remember a schoolboy who slapped you when you refused to go on a date with him. You remember how your best friend called you a dyke and stopped speaking to you.

"Never lead a man on or you'll regret it." He retracts his claws and his black tail follows his enormous body off the path and back into the shrubbery.

You sink down onto the floor of violets. The chest scratches burn or throb, but you can't tell which. Your hands shake as they trace the lines. You're a lesbian. Looking down, there are holes in your shirt but no blood. You're exhausted. You wish you'd known you were a lesbian sooner.

You have to keep going.

* * *

The forest darkens. Tree trunks are thicker than before. The path is so narrow that your elbows scrape trees as you pass. It smells like mouldy earth after rain. Dewy violets squeak against your Docs with each step. Your only company is the sound of your breath.

Realising you haven't checked your phone all day and have no idea what time it is, you pull it from your bag, only to find the battery dead. You're lighter with the knowledge that you're a lesbian, and upon arriving at the cottage, you'll find out who the love of your life is, and you'll settle down, finally happy— not the family's virginal failure!

The thrill of this thought nearly makes you miss the glowing orange eyes further down the path.

"Hi there," you call out, more confident than anyone should be when talking to a wolf. The newfound lesbian status has resulted in high spirits. "Are you alright?"

"I've been waiting for you," the wolf calls out. "A friend told me you slighted him."

"I didn't mean to—honestly. I'm a lesbian, see? He wasn't really my type."

The wolf skulks over, revealing paler fur than the last you'd encountered, it's almost beige. "I know. That's why I came. I want to help. I can be any woman you want me to be. Just say the word."

You think about female celebrities, but aren't really attracted to any of them. "Say the word and what?"

"I will release you from your burden of virginity. Your family will be proud. You'll be able to tell your cousin every saucy detail . . ."

Your skin crawls as though you've stood on an anthill. "I don't know. Surprise me."

The wolf arches its lean back until it cracks. Beige fur bubbles down into pale skin. Pointed toes and slender legs emerge from the wolf's hind legs. As it stretches out, the rest of the body reforms. She shakes her arms with vigour before offering a sultry gaze.

The wolf is Jennifer Lawrence. "My performance in The Hunger Games was remarkable,' she explains. "My

performance with you, however, will be even more so."
Jennifer-wolf bites her lip and pulls you close to her body,
whispering, "What do you want?"

A cold shiver runs down the length of your spine. You try
to say the words "I want you", but they don't come out. All you
want is to be normal.

You begin to cry. "Not this . . . I don't want this . . ."

The she-wolf pushes you away from her and snarls.
"How could you not want me? I try to help and this is what I
get?" She spits venom as tears roll dumbly down your face.
"Not straight? Not a lesbian? You're broken."

You didn't see her transform, but know it must have
happened when she scratches you across the stomach. Shutting
your eyes to the pain, in that moment, you hope she'll gobble
you up and finish the job.

Crying harder now, your chest feels as though a wolf is
sitting on it. You wish you weren't born a broken, sexless
person. You wish you could be fixed. You wish you were
anything other than what you are.

Wiping away tears and forcing a smile, you think about how
great it will feel to learn the truth—whatever it is. Amy called
you a prude, and you can't wait to explain that you're not, that
there is an answer.

Ignoring the pain of your injured stomach, you stand.
Grandad said to believe. You believe in what you know: you

aren't straight, aren't gay, and the path of blossoming purple violets is strewn with wolves. The trail stretches out towards home, but you turn away. Kicking through the suffocating shrubbery, you leave the path for good. You're making your own way to the old lady's house. Maybe the trust Grandad spoke of was about trusting yourself.

* * *

Hanging vines wrap their tendrils around your shoulders, trying to guide you back to the path, but you push past them. Fallen branches block the way, but your Doc Martens stamp over them. There's nothing that can keep you from getting to the house, to Grandmother Love, to answers.

You come to an enormous collapsed tree. Even on its side, its trunk is almost thicker than you are tall. The bark is mottled and scaly. Perfect to grip your shoes into. You grab a nearby vine, pulling it taut. The pressure holds you upright as you put one foot on the trunk. Hoisting yourself up one side, you turn around on the top to lower yourself back down.

The vine snaps. Your knees take the brunt when you hit the ground, landing in a pile of rocks.

Your knees throb. They're imbedded with gravel. They're bleeding. Splinters of bark poke from your arms. You get that hollow feeling when you're being watched.

Shuffling around, you're surprised to see a cottage that wasn't there a moment ago. It has mossy walls of piled grey stone, a sprawling straw roof, and an old timber door, complete with smoking chimney.

The door creaks open, beckoning. Shaking with nervous anticipation and taking a deep breath, you walk inside.

In here, it smells like rot. It's so dark you can hardly see. There's movement in the corner. You step toward it, but it's only a rat.

"Hello?" You call out.

The door closes and you spin on your heel. It's pitch black now. Pulling the matches from your pocket and fumbling, you light one. It sparks and sputters—bright enough to reveal an elderly woman sitting on the edge of a bed.

"I've been waiting for you, little Red," she says.

The match goes out before you can catch her expression. "I was hoping you'd be able to help me."

"Come here. I wish to see you better."

You take a step in her direction. "Are there any lights in here?"

"Come, my child."

Another lit match helps you manoeuvre across the room. Tiny bones litter the floor, and crunch under your shoes. The hairs on your arms stand to attention.

The smell is worse the closer you get to her. The woman grabs your arm with a spindly hand. "Sit down, my dear."

You oblige, and she releases you. Candles ignite themselves on the four posts of the small bedframe, illuminating the mysterious Grandmother Love. She is so frail and wrinkled that you can hardly believe she's alive. Her hair is white and brittle, a tuft of fairy floss atop her head.

"Your grandfather sent you . . . I've been waiting all day."

"Sorry—the path was dangerous. I thought it better to go another way. Grandad thought you could help me. I want to know my future."

"Your future is determined through choice, child." Her voice is a croak. The smell is unbearable. "There is only one which you must make."

Your saliva is stickier than toffee. "I didn't think—um—that it's a choice kind of situation . . . I want an answer of who I am—what I am? It's not really to do with sex—gender, I mean gender. It's everything to do with sex. Um. I want to know how to . . . fix it . . ." You cough, more to give yourself a pause than for necessity in the stench. "Unless . . . Maybe it's not something to fix . . ."

The woman's skinny hand grabs your forearm with surprising strength. "This is your choice. This is your answer."

"What do you mean?"

Her eyes flash red. They seem to grow on her face.

"Your eyes . . . they're huge."

145

"All the better to see you with, my child." The woman smiles, her canines more prominent than ever.

"What's wrong with your teeth?" you say, as you realise the woman is not a woman.

Her skin blisters. She pushes you back onto the bed. Fur sprouts across her body. Her eyes, crimson and menacing, stare out at you from the old lady's face. Her nose elongates into a snout. The wolf growls, inches from you.

You try to move, but the wolf is too heavy. You shove against its chest, but it makes no difference.

"It's okay." The wolf licks through your torn shirt, to the cuts on your stomach. It stings.

You want to throw up.

"The choice is made. This will fix you."

Your heart is pounding. "No!" You push back against the wolf. Trying to push its snout away, it bites down on your palm.

You scream. Blood pours. The wolf stands over you on the bed. There isn't enough air.

"I'm—not—broken." Your gasps surprise even you for a second.

The wolf stretches its mouth wide. Saliva drips onto your cheek.

Your mind drifts back to Grandad's words: try, believe, trust. "Trust me." You reach for a candle on the bedpost. "I don't need to be fixed."

You force the candle into the wolf's face. It howls. The wolf's fur catches alight. It yelps in pain. Panting, you push the wolf onto the floor.

You drag yourself from the bed. Wrenching the door open and shutting it behind you, you run.

You stumble over roots; you kick at shrubbery. The wolf's howl is right behind you. You believed in yourself. The vines don't try to stop you, now. They tangle in your wake. Grandmother Love's fake voice screams for your help. You trust yourself.

Your legs protest each movement. It's hard to breathe. You don't stop. Sunlight slices the canopy ahead. Twigs and leaves crunch under your feet. Eucalypts move out of your way. Ferns sway, letting you pass. You stumble through the last line of trees and—

You're on Jibbon beach.

Alone.

Your breathing is louder than the waves on the shore. The forest behind you has changed. There's nothing lush and green about it anymore. It's the bush. Greying eucalypts and pines, ferns fighting for space and sun and air.

Your shirt is intact. There's no blood. Perspiration drops from your face.

"Oi!"

Pivoting in the direction of the noise, your breath catches.

"Red! It's me! Grandad said you'd be here!"

In the distance Amy is running towards you. You could almost cry with relief. You sit on the sand.

"Oi," Amy says when she's closer. She's panting as though she's been chased through a forest. "Grandad . . . told . . . me to . . . come find . . . you," she says between pants. "He was mad . . . you came . . . alone. Said . . . it's dangerous."

You pat the sand, and she sits. You both stare out at where the river meets the ocean, at the stretch of Cronulla beach across the water. The pine trees look like topiary.

"I wanna say sorry. I lashed out, at Easter. It wasn't cool. I told you I had sex, and you 'oh wow'ed me."

"I didn't—"

"Oi, I'm talking," Amy snaps. "I was mad because it was important to me and you didn't care."

"I—"

"Shut up, I'm apologising. It wasn't okay that I threw you to the wolves. I'm sorry."

"I really don't like wolves," you say quietly. Amy's staring at her feet. You trust, believe, and decide to try.

"Look," you say. "I don't want you to think I don't care about you and your sexing or whatever. It's not that . . . it makes me so uncomfortable. Like sick to my stomach."

Amy raises her eyebrows. "That's weird."

"This is why I don't tell you anything!"

"Wait, shit. Sorry. I have no filter." Amy scratches her head. "So, what, sex is gross to you?"

"I guess?"

"I mean, when you take out all the pleasure-y stuff, like, then it's pretty gross," Amy says generously. "Like body parts and juices—"

You make a loud gagging noise and Amy cuts herself off.

"Yeah, that's like how I see it," you say. "But I don't get past how gross it is. Ever."

The roar of a speedboat catches your attention. You both watch it drive from the river and out into the ocean.

"I didn't know I knew anyone like that . . ." Amy admits. "But like, if that's you, that's you. I'm still here. We just won't talk about sex. No prob."

For the first time in your life, some of the weight on your shoulders lifts. Someone's heard you, they've listened. They care.

"Sorry you haven't felt like you could mention it before," Amy adds.

"I didn't think you'd believe me."

Amy shakes her head, "I trust you to know yourself. I'll always believe you, Red."

"Oh."

Amy squeezes your hand.

"Do you reckon . . . there's other people out there like me?"

"Well, duh." Your look is so incredulous that Amy keeps talking. "You're ace, right? Asexual? There's a whole community of people—there's even a literary journal."

Your eyes have never been so wide. "What?"

"I did a uni assignment on it," she says, nodding. "Basic gist is that aces don't experience sexual desire or attraction. But that's the bottom line. They can still have relationships and get married and stuff. Like, I know our family craps on and on about it, but sex isn't really the be all and end all." Amy looks a little smug over knowing more about your potential sexual orientation than you do, but it's better than her I've-had-sex-so-I'm-better-than-you look so you let it slide.

You're a bit distracted by what she's saying, anyway.

"Surely you've googled it before." Amy raises her eyebrows.

"Google said I have a disorder!"

"Common misconception," Amy says smoothly. She stops herself from adding her next nugget of information when she catches sight of your face. "Are you okay?"

You lean against her and let your tears fall. For the first time, it feels cathartic, not hopeless. "I thought I was alone."

The speedboat crosses back through the mouth of the Port Hacking. A girl on board shrieks with laughter.

"No one is, Red," Amy says. "They just think they are."

LITTLE RED

Resting your head against Amy's shoulder, your smile. You don't fully know if you're asexual or not. You don't know much more about it than a sentence. You don't know why you ever doubted Grandad—magic is in all kinds of places, you just need to know where to look.

About the Author:

Lucy Fox is a queer and disabled writer currently living on Dharawal land. She holds a BCA (Honours) in Creative Writing and can be found in Imprint Magazine, Baby Teeth Arts Journal, the Emma Press and on Twitter @LucyFox96.

Northern Queensland. The part of Australia that
your mother warned you about.

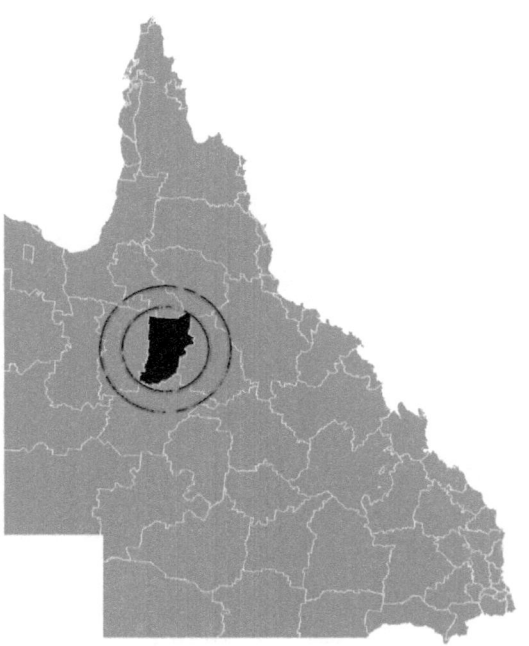

GHOSTS OF THE INLAND SEA

Geraldine Borella

Last night's whisky sits sour in Professor Duncan Tiller's stomach as he steps onto the university minibus. His head pounds and his mouth is as dry as the outback town he's en route to. The eight hour trip west from Cairns to the dig at Richmond should be enough to sleep it off, as long as Emily doesn't keep him awake with her incessant chatter and ridiculous meme-sharing. He'd been smart with this one though, suggesting an open relationship from the start. If only he'd thought of that back in Birmingham. Maybe he'd still be there, heading the Palaeontology Department.

Easing into his seat, guarding his head from bumps and jolts, he sighs. He should've controlled himself last night, but losing out on the research grant was a kick to the teeth he hadn't seen coming, and his old friend Chivas Regal had called.

"This is gonna be so much fun," chirps Emily, plonking into the seat across the aisle.

Tiller's smile is half-hearted as he leans towards her. "Mightn't be such a good idea to sit together though, hey?" he whispers. "We don't want people to get the wrong idea." He nods in the direction of the other students, then grimaces at the reverberating thud the movement creates.

Emily pouts and shrugs. "Sure, whatever." She saunters towards the back of the bus and Tiller sighs with relief. He doesn't need another 'situation' right now, one more black mark against his academic record.

She's right though. The trip *will* be fun, given the recent fossil find out in Richmond—the lower jawbone of a huge pterosaur with an estimated seven metre wingspan; a veritable giant of the Cretaceous inland sea, found by a local fossicker and handed into the museum in town. *Christ!* If only he'd been given the inside information on *that* find, instead of it going to a rival uni. Would've made his career.

Still, where there's one, there'll be others—other fossil species and other academic-stature cash-cows. The trick is to be in the right place at the right time, looking over the shoulder of some witless second year who wouldn't know the difference between a fossil and a concretion.

"Is that everyone?" asks PhD student Phil Everett, consulting his clipboard. Tiller had strongarmed him and his fellow PhD candidate, Marta Deimel, into coming along to help. Who else was going to cook, clean and organise the rabble? Of course, neither wanted to come, both asserting the field trip didn't align with their areas of doctoral research, and that they were flat out with work, study and tutoring. But Tiller flexed his doctoral-committee muscle and like magic, commitments were shuffled, diary spaces opened up. *Funny that*, thinks Tiller with a smirk.

"One more!" calls a voice at the door. The minibus rocks as a newcomer mounts the steps, and Tiller groans. It's Jonathan Baumgart. *What's he doing here?*

"Hey, Prof B," says Everett, fist-bumping Baumgart in far too familiar a fashion for Tiller's liking. "Thanks for stepping up at such short notice. Marta said to say thanks too." Tiller fumes, noticing Marta is indeed missing. Why hadn't she rung? He could have arranged someone else. *Anyone else.*

"Yeah, sorry to hear about her gran," says Baumgart, and the men exchange a grim nod. "Terrible news."

"That's it then," says Everett as Professor Baumgart makes his way down the narrow aisle. "All twelve of us, present and accounted for."

"Howdy partner." Baumgart tips his Akubra hat to Tiller. "S'pose Marta's told you I'm her substitute?"

Tiller clears his throat. "Yes . . . of course. Thanks for agreeing to help out."

"No problem." Baumgart winks, kicking off the throb in Tiller's head once more.

He hates to say it, but it wouldn't look good to come across as a sore loser. "Oh, congratulations, by the way." He stretches his dry lips into something resembling a smile.

"Cheers," says Baumgart. "And commiserations for missing out. Better luck next time, huh?"

Tiller nods and Baumgart gives him a patronising pat on the shoulder, then continues on down the aisle.

Must he stick the boot in?

"Anyone sitting here, young lady?"

Emily awards Baumgart the same coquettish giggle she normally reserves for him. "All yours, Prof B."

What the devil?

As the bus winds its way up through the rainforest corridors of the Kuranda Range and on to the Atherton Tablelands, Tiller keeps his attention focussed to the front. Every sound from behind rankles, plunging daggers into already gaping wounds. Perhaps he should have endured Emily's inane chatter, after all. But it's too late to change all that, so he sinks low in his seat, closes his eyes, and hopes for sweet, sweet oblivion.

* * *

When the bus pulls up in Ravenshoe, Tiller visits the bakery, lured by the smell. *Hmmm, pastries, coffee, ham and cheese toasties.* He buys a flat white for zing, and a cheese and bacon pie to line his queasy stomach, then heads to the tables outside.

"Highest town in Queensland, this is," says Baumgart. He's at an adjacent table, sitting amongst students. Pulling on a pretend-smoke, finger and thumb to his lips, he winks and adds, "If you know what I mean." He gets a few cheap laughs for his effort. *Juvenile!*

"It's a reference to geology, Baumgart," says Tiller. "Not pharmacology."

"It's a joke, Tills," Baumgart shoots back. "Lighten up, would you. Ha ha—get it?"

"Once you've eaten, get back on the bus," Everett announces before Tiller can respond. He's sticking to the planned itinerary.

Next stop: a dip in Innot Hot Springs. It sounded good on paper, but now Tiller wishes they could keep driving. Plunging his pasty white body into piping hot mineral springs, with gym junkie Baumgart prancing about in tight swimming trunks—or dick-togs in the colonial parlance—isn't so appealing.

Still, maybe Emily will see him for the poser he is!

Still, the mineral springs are refreshing. Patches of cool mix in amongst the warmth, and Tiller finds it restorative. He splashes his face and feels almost human again. It's a surprising whisky-night reset, and he's gifted with a whole new outlook.

Even better, Emily chooses to join him, dressed in her red bikini that covers only the important bits.

"It's so nice, isn't it?" she says, reclining on the sand, leaning on her forearms. Her head falls back and the ends of her long blonde hair dip beneath the water. She closes her eyes, basking in the sun. Tiller's gaze traces shadows and curves, from the gracefulness of her neck to the sweet protrusion of clavicle and further down to the dewy skin that plumps out from—

"Mind if I join you?" says Baumgart, lowering into the pool without waiting for an answer.

"Ummm, sure," says Tiller with reluctance. He splashes his face once more, and inhales.

"What the hell's that, Tills?" asks Baumgart, using the overly familiar nickname Tiller abhors. "What?"

"There! On your forehead." Baumgart leans forward, squinting, and then snorts. "Is that . . . hair dye?" He laughs loud, as Tiller swipes and checks his hand. Black dye stains his fingers, and he jumps out of the pool in search of his towel, as embarrassed as a schoolboy at a swimming carnival, caught with a sneaky erection.

* * *

The bus rolls into the Lakeview Caravan Park in Richmond around 5pm, after a stop in Charters Towers, an outback town with a history in gold mining. It's a fleeting stop but Tiller makes a mental note to come back, to linger longer at a later date. Maybe with Emily?

The caravan park sits on a grassy expanse that overlooks a lake—Lake Fred Tritton—and is surprisingly busy, packed with grey nomads and young families in camper trailers. Everett and Baumgart set to organising tents and sleeping gear, while Tiller heads off to the local hotel.

"I need to square things away with the catering," he explains.

"Aaah, so you're a blister then?" Baumgart shares an eyebrow raise with Everett.

"A blister?"

"They turn up after the work's done."

Everett fails to stifle a laugh, and Tiller shoots him a warning glare. He wants his doctorate awarded, doesn't he?

When he gets to the Federal Palace Hotel, a huge double-storey colonial timber structure that houses a large horseshoe-shaped bar, beer garden, restaurant lounge and accommodation, he marvels at the difference between English and Australian pubs. No fox, goose, hare or hound to be seen in a name here. No beautiful old stonework or exposed wooden beams either, at least not out in the rural towns. Still, the lager's cold and flowing and that's all that matters right now.

"I'll take a pint of Great Northern please," says Tiller, ordering the beer favoured by the locals.

"How ya goin'?" asks an older gent dressed in a flannelette shirt, jeans, a worn-out Akubra. He's a barfly, thinks Tiller, going by the impressive bulge of his keg-sized beer belly.

"Evening," says Tiller.

"Ah, you're a Pom, hey?" says Keg-belly.

"Yes, yes I am." Tiller wipes the frothy head off his upper lip and nods. "Living in Cairns right now though."

"Shit, that musta been a culture shock, climate-wise I mean. Good ole hot and humid FNQ. Melted your lily white arse when ya landed, I'll bet."

"Yes . . . it was a bit of a shock," says Tiller, the man's vernacular causing his teeth to ache. "But I'm getting used to it now."

"This always helps," says Keg-belly, lifting his pint of beer. "Keeps ya hydrated." He drains the glass, places it on the counter and winks at Tiller. "Still a tad thirsty. Might need to get meself another, I reckon."

"Indeed," says Tiller, assembling a smile of sorts. Call him a cultural snob and a phonological pedant, but to hear the Queen's English mangled so upset him. He'd had this discussion with expats before. They'd argue on the side of the local ocker, calling them 'quaint' and 'salt-of-the-earth', the type to give you the shirt off their back, despite their languid labourer lingo. But Tiller would respond with a treatise about maintaining standards and not letting one rotten apple spoil the barrel.

"Whatcha doin' out here then?" asks Keg-belly.

"I'm a professor of palaeontology," Tiller spouts. "Taking students on a field trip." Informing others of his credentials never got old, and he enjoyed delivering them to plebs like this one, if only to watch the subsequent look of awe veer towards intimidation.

"Aw yeah?" says the man. "Ya checkin' out the quarry where Len found the pterosaur fossil, are ya?"

"Len?"

"Yeah, he's me mate. We fossick together from time to time. Found quite a few treasures over the years, we have, but Len struck gold on this one. Lucky bugger."

"Have you found anything interesting yourself?"

"Shit yeah," says Keg-belly. "Found some belemnites and parts of an ichthyosaur—a Platypterygius australis, would you believe? Probably nothing compared to what *you've* found though, hey? Bein' a professor and all."

Tiller chuckles to cover his embarrassment, not wanting to admit that he's never discovered anything of significance himself, has only ever assisted others with their finds. That this barfly has done so jars him more than any mangling of language ever could.

"I've had my share," he lies.

Keg-belly sculls the refill placed before him and sets the empty glass down on the bar-mat, then gets up to go. "Well, good luck out there. But watch yourselves. Things can go south pretty quick, and you're a long way from help."

"This *isn't* my first field trip," blurts Tiller, not even bothering to hide his disdain.

"You've come prepared then, have ya?"

"I know all about the dangers of the outback: the snakes, the spiders, the dingos and such."

"Aw yeah, fair enough." Keg-belly crosses his arms over his chest with an amused nod.

"Flash flooding," adds Tiller, as though expecting it to be pointed out.

"Yep," says Keg-belly, his expression sobering. "There's that. And maybe a few other things too."

* * *

After dinner at the pub, Tiller retires early. The others have stayed on for a few more drinks, but with Baumgart lurking, ready to one-up him at any opportunity, Tiller wants to be fresh and on his game when the sun peeks over the horizon in the morning. On his return to the park he finds his tent still in its bag, a note rubber-banded around it: *Enjoy your night-time erection, Tills.* He snorts, imagining Everett and Baumgart sniggering like schoolboys as they wrote it. *Tossers!*

Undeterred, he grabs the spare keys to the minibus, tosses the tent-bag inside and stretches out on the backseat, laying his sleeping bag out like a blanket.

* * *

The morning hits hot, the first rays of sun spearing in through the minibus windows, and Tiller jumps up, ready to roll. As he exits the bus, a spike of irritation harpoons—Baumgart is up and about already, sipping coffee at a picnic table.

"Morning Princess," he says with a mocking salute.

Tiller refuses to react; he nods then does the rounds of the tents, waking everyone up.

After a quick breakfast of tinned fruit, instant coffee and breakfast bars, tents are dismantled and the group are on their way, Tiller barking orders.

"Talk about militant," jokes Baumgart, as he climbs on the bus. "Should we call Prof Tills The Supreme Leader?" He looks around and is rewarded with sniggers and nods.

Tiller doesn't bite back. Instead, he turns to address Everett. "Let's go, before the day disappears altogether."

Out at the dig site, an hour and a half north-west of Richmond, the bus pulls up and Tiller gets cracking. He scouts the sparse vegetation for a suitable area to make camp. "Tents, kitchen annexe, chairs, tables, shower and toilet cubicle, let's get it all up and ready to go. Baumgart, you can dig the long-drop." He revels in the joy of handing over the post-hole digger, but Baumgart doesn't flinch; he grabs the implement and heads away in search of soft ground.

When the camp is up, Everett—with the help of a few students—makes ham and salad sandwiches. They take camp chairs over to the steep embankment to catch a breeze and look down onto the murky brown river below. It's a fair way from the camp site, but Tiller wants to forestall any chance of being caught in a flash flood. Baumgart had argued with him about it, scoffing at the idea of a flash flood at this time of year, but Tiller stood firm. Obtaining clearance to camp at the dig site had been tough enough without needing to call for rescue.

"Let's get to it," says Tiller, once lunch is over.

The students have an assignment to complete while digging for fossils, and all Tiller has to do is look over shoulders and provide academic advice.

"Is this anything, Dunc?" asks Emily. She's kneeling by sheared off plates of limestone dug from the dry clay, pointing to a depression.

Tiller glances around. *Has anyone heard her?* "No," says Tiller. "Keep digging." And in a whisper, "Call me Professor out here, Em. We don't want any problems now, do we?"

"Oh, soz, babes." Emily flashes that smile of hers and he feels ridiculous, like a lecherous old man.

* * *

There's little to show at the end of Day One, apart from sore muscles and sunburn. Tiller calls it a night after dinner, unable to listen to Baumgart's posturing any longer.

He'd monopolised the entire conversation, droning on about dig sites he's worked at—in South Africa and Mexico—and is now spruiking about his grant win. The students ask Baumgart questions with a hero-worship gaze, and disregard Tiller altogether; he's an old man at a nightclub, annoying and irrelevant, and he's had enough. He winks at Emily, and she smiles. They'd shared a moment earlier, while collecting washing-up water, Tiller dropping a hint about hating to have to sleep alone. He hopes she's picked it up.

Emily doesn't visit that night though, and even worse, he hears her giggles coming from a tent nearby. He sticks his head out to listen. *Baumgart's tent!* His self-absorbed drone is followed by Emily's muffled reply. Zipping up the tent flap, Tiller slumps back down on his stretcher but the noise filters through. He grabs his earplugs and shoves them in. Emily hasn't taken his hint, or perhaps disregarded it altogether. But then, he's got no right to be angry. They've agreed on an open relationship. She can see whomever she chooses, *when*ever she chooses. *But a poser like Baumgart? Out here? Come on.*

* * *

On Day Three, Emily and her field-trip partner, Mei, make a significant discovery. Baumgart is first on the scene, strutting over before Tiller can get there.

"Tooth sockets!" he exclaims. "Be careful girls. We don't want to ruin anything. Step back, step back!"

"They're small." Tiller kneels to assess the situation. "A baby of some sort."

"It's a pterosaur!" says Baumgart. "Can't you see? It's the skull of a baby pterosaur."

"I don't think we should jump to conclusions." His obnoxious rival is right but Tiller doesn't want him anywhere near this, trying to claim ownership.

"I'm telling you, man, that's what it is!"

Baumgart gathers tools to excavate the area, ordering students around and overstepping his bounds. Tiller wants to rein him in, but the horse has already bolted, taken off with the cart, and he's in danger of being tipped out of the driver's seat altogether.

"What a find, hey?" he says, trying to regain a semblance of control. "A baby pterosaur. Emily, you and Mei will co-author my paper." He nods at the girls and flashes them a magnanimous smile

Baumgart ignores him, jotting in a notebook, then begins to take photos.

"I'll sort that, thanks Baumgart," says Tiller. "You go help Everett make lunch."

"No, no, my expertise is needed here," he replies.

"I'd rather document it, since it's *my* field trip group. My course, my discovery, my paper. You know how it is, old chap."

"It's science, man. No-one owns it." He gestures at the group. "In fact, if anything, we all own it. Isn't that right, guys?"

"Interesting point," says Emily, and Mei nods. The other students make noises of agreement and stare at Tiller.

"We should *all* be co-authors," says Mei. "It's only fair."

Tiller frowns. "But that's not really how things—"

"Unless, of course, you feel the need to take *all* the glory," says Baumgart, with a derisive snort.

Tiller wants to punch him. Baumgart has taken the moral high ground, inciting mutiny to boot. He won't stand for it, not from a bell-end like Baumgart! "This discovery *must* be revealed at the right time, and in the right manner. It *must* be given the respect it deserves." He nods at the gathered group and focuses on Baumgart. "Shall we call this a gentleman's agreement then?"

Mei snorts and glances at Emily. "Well that rules us out then."

"Huh?" Tiller frowns, confused.

"Yes, good point, Mei. Let's call it a gentle*person's* agreement," says Baumgart, extending his hand to Tiller.

"Right . . . gentleperson . . . yes," says Tiller. He shakes on it, then addresses the group. "Let's get this baby out of the ground then."

They set to task, scraping with claw hammer and brush, unearthing the fossil from the layers of limestone, sandstone and clay.

It takes all day for the skull to emerge, and boy, is it a sight to behold. It's a major find, one Tiller doesn't want to share with Baumgart, and in his tent that night, he considers how best to play this.

* * *

Around 3am, Tiller gets up to relieve himself and bumps into Everett, who looks shaken.

"What's wrong?" he asks.

"Didn't you hear that?" Everett glances around, staring in the direction of the granite hills that line the basin plain.

"Hear what?"

"That high-pitched screech." Everett shudders. "A godawful sound."

"Dingoes?"

"It wasn't a howl though. It was a definite screech. And I saw lights, too."

"What sort of lights. Headlights?" Tiller then scoffs. "Or Min-Min lights?"

"No . . . it was more like . . . I don't know . . . an aurora."

"Don't be daft, Everett. We're in the tropics. That only happens near the poles."

"I know, I know . . . I . . ." He rubs his arms, despite the mild temperature. "Something's wrong, Professor. I don't know what but . . . something seems off."

"What are you talking about?"

"I can't explain it. It's just a feeling I get. That maybe we shouldn't be here."

Tiller snorts. "Might be time to lay off the mushrooms, hey?"

Everett stares at Tiller for a long moment. "Forget it," he mutters, as he turns and wanders off in the direction of his tent. Tiller smiles and shakes his head. *What nonsense.*

Under the bright full moon, he picks a spot to water the vegetation, then heads back to bed.

* * *

At the end of Day Five, as the last rays of sun dip beneath the volcanic hills, darkening the orange-pink sky, Tiller plants his hands on his hips and surveys the dig.

"This is big!" he says. "Huge!"

The baby pterosaur fossil has been unearthed, pristine from crest to toothy jaw.

Baumgart pulls the sat phone from his back pocket, then struts away from the spotlit dig-zone.

"What are you doing? Who gave you permission to use the sat phone? It's only for emergencies," Tiller yells, but Baumgart doesn't answer. "Baumgart, who are you calling? I hope you're not going back on our agreement."

". . . yes, a significant fossil find . . . it's the skull of a baby pterosaur."

"Baumgart! Who the *fuck* are you talking to?"

Baumgart chuckles, and turns his back on Tiller. ". . . yeah, I guess it *could* be the baby of the adult that was found . . . who can really say? But it'd make an emotive angle for your story, for sure."

"You're talking to the *press*?"

"That's right, Professor Jonathan Baumgart, spelt B . . . A . . . U. . ."

"You selfish prick!" Tiller lunges, tackling him to the ground.

"Oomph!" The phone flies from Baumgart's hand.

Fists find their mark, landing in Baumgart's face and ribs. Baumgart grabs Tiller around the middle and they roll about in the dusty ground. Kicking. Punching. Wrestling. Emily screams.

"Stop it, you two!" Everett drops his torch and jumps in to pull Tiller off Baumgart. A student steps in to create a barrier.

"Okay, okay!" Tiller pushes out of Everett's grasp, brushing dust and dried clay off his pants. "I'll stop, all right."

By the light of the LED lamps, Tiller eyes Baumgart, waiting for him to make another move. Baumgart squints, then turns and runs towards the fossilised skull. He picks it up, cradling it like a football.

"No, you fucking don't!" yells Tiller, launching at Baumgart. Baumgart turns and runs for goal, but trips and falls. The skull hits hard rock and smashes.

Before Tiller or Baumgart, or any of the others can react, a terrifying sound—a piercing screech like no other—echoes around the basin. It's followed by a deep rumble and roar, like that of a jumbo jet, and Tiller peers in the direction of the granite hills. *What the hell's going on?* His heart hammers, and his mouth goes bone dry, as the demonic screech sounds again.

"What the fuck *is* that?" yells Baumgart. He turns in circles, searching for the source.

"It's the same noise I heard the other night," Everett cries. "I told you, Tiller . . . I fucking told you something wasn't right . . ."

The rumble gets louder and water rushes in, gushing forth from between the hills in a translucent spectral mass.

"Run!" yells Tiller. "Run for higher ground."

The flap of wings beats down from above and the dreadful screeching grows louder. The sound rips through him like a thousand fingernails scraped down a blackboard. He runs towards the embankment, lost in the dark shadow of whatever coasts overhead. A few metres in front, Baumgart screams; he's been scooped up, captured in the jaws of a dragon-like creature. Tiller gapes, squinting at the massive beast. *Surely not? It can't be!* It looks like an adult pterosaur, glowing golden, the image flickering in and out. It lifts Baumgart high in the sky then flings him away, dashing his body against a mound of granite rock. *I must be going mad,* thinks Tiller. *This can't be happening.*

The raging water continues to rise, whisking screaming students away. Tiller is swept up too, and swims hard against the pull, struggling to keep his head above the surface. *Where's Emily?* He can't see her anywhere. He glances about, and cops a mouthful. It's salty, like gulping the sea. Nearby, Everett slips under and struggles, caught in the slashing metre-long jaws of an ichthyosaur. *Fuck me!*

Salty water fills Tiller's lungs as he submerges. He's a long way down, kicking his way to the surface, surrounded by glowing dinosaurs of the deep. Large cephalopodic ancestors of squid and octopus dart and scurry about, as schools of elongated armoured fish—*Richmondichthys sweeti*, he notes—swim by. Shark-like predators with luminescent teeth gulp giant clams and crunch on neon green turtles, while iridescent ichthyosaurs and plesiosaurs glide past on either side. Coral shimmers and swirls, mesmerising Tiller with rich colour— fluorescing pink, purple, orange and green—and alien shapes of tubes and rings. But he has to get out of the water, before he becomes fish food.

Where the hell is Emily? He should try to help her, help the others too. But he can't think about that. Not right now. It's everyone for themselves.

He fights his way to the surface, the glow of ancient creatures guiding him in the right direction. They don't touch him. They leave him alone. Is it a sign? A sign that he's favoured? That *he's* the rightful owner of the fossil? That he was all along? The baby skull was broken, by Baumgart and his selfishness, but the rest of the skeleton is no doubt still intact, hidden beneath the clay. If he survives, he can excavate, unearth the treasure and take a bow. After enduring all this, he deserves every second of the success coming his way.

Breaking through, he scrambles onto a rocky escarpment and gasps for air. He splutters and coughs as he surveys the landscape. Near the top of a granite hill bordering the basin, he gazes down onto the luminous inland sea, scanning for survivors. There are bodies washed up on rocks, one draped in a tree. *God, Emily must be dead too. Maybe they all are?* He needs to call for help, a search party to look for survivors and find the bodies scattered along the length of the plain.

It seems a lot right now. Far too much to process. He rests for a moment and wonders how he's going to explain it all, until his thoughts are banished by the beat of wings from behind. A hellish screech precedes the swooping attack and Tiller is lifted up, right leg trapped in the mouth of the pterosaur. Sharp teeth spear through the flesh of his thigh, delivering hot searing pain. It's excruciating, worsened by him flailing and jolting about. Screams fly from his mouth. He doesn't recognise them as his own—so high-pitched and helpless; so child-like and insignificant. They echo and taunt as the crested pterosaur glides over the sea, tossing him about like a play-toy. He falls and tumbles; snapshots of stars, moon and sky flicker through his field of vision.

This is it, he thinks. *This is how it ends.*

Waves and rocky outcrops rise to meet him and he welcomes the prospect of a quick release. But the pterosaur circles and snaps him up once more, catching him around the middle. Heavy jaws crunch through vertebrae as though they're nothing but fragile bird bones. Tiller sobs and whispers to a God he's never bothered to get to know. But it's too late for introductions now. It's over. As he fades in and out, at last able to let go, he marvels at the calls of the plesiosaurs that breach the ghostly waters far below.

About the Author:

Geraldine Borella writes fiction for children, young adults and adults. She lives in Yungaburra, Far North Queensland, Australia, on Ngadjon-Jii land. Her stories and poems have been published by Deadset Press, IFWG Publishing, Busybird Publishing, Celapene Press, Wombat Books/Rhiza Edge, AHWA/Midnight Echo, Antipodean SF (online and in podcast), and Raven & Drake Books. She has a story published in Spawn – Weird Horror Tales About Pregnancy, Birth and Babies, a horror anthology that won the 2021 AHWA Shadows Award for Best Edited Work.

You can find more about her at https://geraldineborella.com/about/ https://www.facebook.com /geraldineb4/ and at https://mobile.twitter.com/geraldineborel2

Between Ridgehaven and Paradise lies the Hope Valley Reservoir. More than big enough to lose yourself in.

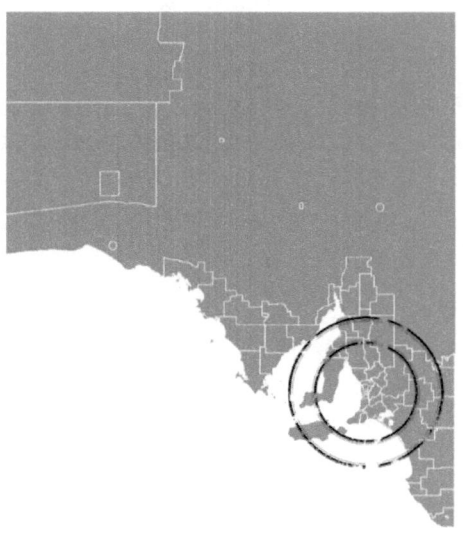

THE VALLEY

Sarah Jane Justice

The sound of the alarm reached Toby as if it were submerged in an ocean during a thunderstorm. He could tell he was lying flat, and he was able to wiggle his fingers and toes. The effort of it left him even weaker, ready to give up the fight and remain motionless.

The stress ball hit him hard enough to snap his eyes open, although its squishy texture ensured that his only pain stemmed from being forced awake.

"Get up." Chloe clapped her hands over Toby's head. "You'll be late again."

He heard the deep groan fill the room before he realised that it was coming from his own mouth. He stretched in a dramatic motion, only to be hit by another soft projectile.

"Up," Chloe repeated. "Christ, Toby, am I your girlfriend or your mother?"

"Okay, okay." Toby sat up. "Would rather not blur the line between those two things, babe."

Chloe flung another cushion in his direction. She grumbled loud enough to make her point clear, but Toby could always tell when she was trying not to laugh.

"Another morning in Paradise," he yawned, pulling himself out of bed.

"I'm not sure I would have agreed to move here if I knew you'd be making that joke every single day."

"What point is there in moving to a suburb named Paradise if you can't make that joke every single day?" Toby grinned, finally finding the motivation to climb out of bed. He grabbed Chloe around the waist, leaning closer as she turned away to hide her smile. "Did you hear about the new parking lot at the interchange? Excellent paving job. Someone should-"

"Should write to Joni Mitchell," Chloe finished the joke for him. "As I said. You're so predictable."

"Being predictable is a good thing," Toby insisted. "You'd know straight away if I was replaced by a clone."

Chloe picked up a bath towel and flung it in his direction. "Clones. You're going to be making up nonsense about clones now, are you?" She sighed. "First you try to tell me that you failed your uni placement because you were attacked by emus-"

"That was true!" Toby jumped to reply. "I'm telling you, again, that story was true, just it was pretty hard to get footage given-"

"Stop," Chloe laughed. "I've heard it too many times. You're so full of it."

Toby held back his argument and bent over to pick up the towel. He yawned as Chloe gave him a gentle shove towards the bathroom.

"Are you right to walk to work today?" She pushed past him. "I'd like to take the car, if that's okay with you."

"Yeah, should be fine," he muttered. "Long as it doesn't rain."

"It better not." Chloe jangled the keys in her hand. "We're trying this new method of waterproofing, and rain would be just what we don't need today."

"Yeah, cool." Toby yawned again. "Good stuff."

"Management shipped in this new type of spray-on rubber coating," she muttered. "I'll be picking it up on the way."

"Sounds delicious."

"Toby." Chloe sighed.

"What?" he argued, pulling her in for a kiss before she opened the front door. "I'm listening."

She stared at him, doing her best to appear stern. Toby retaliated with an innocent shrug, shifting into a silly face he knew would always make Chloe laugh.

"I'll just tell you again tonight." She shook her head. "Hurry up and get ready for work."

"Yeah, yeah." Toby waved. "Have fun. Love you."

Chloe checked the contents of her purse, counting the coins before blowing him a kiss and heading out the door. Toby stretched as he turned around, fighting the temptation to go back to bed. Forcing one foot in front of the other, he stumbled into the bathroom. As the engine of the ute kicked into gear, he peeked out of the small, frosted window to watch Chloe drive away. Checking the time on his phone, he sighed and started running the shower.

* * *

Walking up the Linear Park trail, Toby hummed under his breath without realising he was doing it. Ever since he'd realised that the name of his workplace fit perfectly to the tune of 'Highway to Hell', the song had become an unbreakable part of his commute. As soon as the words 'Highbury Hotel' landed in his brain, the tune began, whether he liked it or not.

Toby walked through the park knowing that he was about to be hit by constant chatter, bland music, and endless ringing pokie machines. With that in mind, he walked without headphones. Immersed in the serenity of rushing water and birdsong, he could almost forget the busy peak-hour roads that surrounded the trail. It was rare that he admitted how much he valued those few quiet moments, but he often took a pause just before the trail ended.

To get to the Highbury Hotel, Toby had no other option but to turn onto Lower North-East Road as it snaked up the hill. Towards the end, the path offered a pristine view of the Hope Valley Reservoir, but it was tainted by the inescapable sounds of traffic. Trying to block out the busy engines and blaring horns, Toby turned away from the road to look down at the reservoir. With a deep sigh, he breathed in the last morsel of peace that he would find until he finished his shift.

"I'm at the Highbury Ho-"

Toby's off-key singing was cut off as his feet slipped in a patch of mud. He grabbed the fence to steady himself, and groaned as he saw the fresh brown-green stain splashed onto his pants.

"Bloody laundry day again," he muttered. "Suburban groundhog day."

In a wave of frustration, he aimed a steel-toed kick at the mud. Despite not being hit, the moss beneath the puddle lurched out of the way, a bright green bubble popping as if it were angry. Toby stopped in his tracks, staring at the ground until his vision blurred enough for him to convince himself that he'd imagined it.

* * *

Still humming, Toby strode through the pub's entrance and pushed his way behind the bar.

"Staff only, sorry mate." Alex shook his head with a smirk.

"Yeah, think you're funny, hey."

"Funnier than you." Alex shrugged, throwing a polishing cloth in Toby's direction. "Not that that's any kind of challenge."

Toby made a face, but caught the cloth without any further comment. He took a deep breath, walking through the first steps of his work routine.

"I hit that running track around the reservoir this morning," Alex flexed. "Valley of Hope, indeed. I'll be marathon-ready in no time."

"Whatever you reckon," Toby laughed. "You're jogging in Hope Valley, but you're living in Dream Valley with that attitude."

"Yeah, okay," Alex scoffed. "How's that teaching degree going? Finished yet?"

Toby looked over his shoulder to see one of the pub's most regular customers sidling up to the bar. Grateful for the distraction, he stepped forward and grabbed a pint glass.

"Pint of pale?" he offered, spinning the glass in his hand. "Nice day for it."

"That's the one." Jimmy smacked a bank note onto the counter. "How's that degree of yours coming along? Teaching, wasn't it?"

Alex burst into laughter behind him. He focused on pouring the beer.

"Good on you." Jimmy raised his glass without noticing that Toby hadn't answered him. "God, hell of a thing, that, isn't it?"

Toby swivelled around to the TV behind the bar. A helicopter camera panned across the Hope Valley Reservoir before the scene cut to an image of a young woman. It was the type of picture that was always used for missing persons reports, showing her happy and smiling with a small dog in her arms.

"She might still be alive," Jimmy frowned. "No-one's found a body yet."

"Yeah, wow," Alex whistled. "That's rough. Right near here too, by the looks."

"Yup." Jimmy shook his head before taking a swig from his glass. "All the more reason for this, I suppose."

Toby heard Alex mutter something under his breath, but the words blurred around his ears. He read over the monthly discounts until they became a meaningless mantra, a prayer to Jack Daniels, the patron saint of piss-ups. The thought made him laugh, and it was just enough to free his mind from speculations about missing persons. Repeating the mantra under his breath, Toby returned his focus to work.

* * *

The buses had stopped running by the time Toby's shift finished, but he was more than happy to walk. He counted his steps down Lower North-East Road until it led him to the

Torrens, and with it, the entrance to Linear Park. The quiet air was even fresher on the walk home. Scented with river water and eucalyptus, it overpowered the lingering bar smell that clung to his clothes. In daylight hours, he shared the path with joggers and dog-walkers, but after dark, he had the place to himself.

As his thoughts slowed, Toby found it hard to forget the face of the woman who'd gone missing. The conversation with Jimmy and Alex played back to him on a loop, retelling details he wished he hadn't heard. He took a deep breath and picked up a pebble, tossing it into the air a few times before he sent it out towards the river. It bounced twice before it sank, dropping below the surface with a stout, satisfying plop.

In the dark, Toby wasn't expecting to see the ripple that followed. The bright green colour grabbed his attention, glowing as it bubbled to the surface. The water frothed and popped, gurgling loud enough that he could hear it from the path. Acting against the internal voice that was screaming at him to run, he crept closer. The oozing green substance pulsed like a lava lamp, and he couldn't help but watch as it spread across the water's surface. The dripping goo swayed back and forth until it shot forward with a sudden lurch, gripping the banks with a force that crushed the weeds.

Toby jumped, then ducked behind a bush when he heard the low rumble of an engine. He was glad for the cover of overgrown grass when he saw the matte black SUV. It crawled along the path at the pace of a cat approaching prey, and Toby crouched as low to the ground as he could. He fumbled his phone out of his pocket and fought back a curse when he discovered that it was flat.

Focused on staying motionless, he watched as the car stopped at the river's edge. Two men climbed out, though he could barely make them out. They moved as if they had spent their whole lives training to appear invisible, wearing long gloves and masks that covered their faces. Toby squinted to follow their movements as one of them scraped a patch of neon-green moss into a black container and jammed it shut. In one swift motion, the man ducked aside while his partner pulled out a spray nozzle and blasted it towards the river. The water's surface exploded with grey foam, and spread until the bubbling green substance was covered.

Toby held his breath and pulled his shirt over his face. The lingering bar smell wasn't pleasant, but it was far preferable to the burning chemical odour that was wafting up from the water. Staying hunched down, he looked at the protective equipment both men were wearing and thanked his lucky stars that he was crouched upwind.

When the full width of the Torrens had been sprayed, the two men climbed back into the car. Toby watched, not willing to move a muscle, until they drove back down the path without turning on the headlights.

* * *

As he closed the door behind him, Toby let out a breath so loud that he almost spooked himself. Still shaking, he checked to make sure the lock was secure before he peeked out the window. The street was populated only with parked cars and mailboxes, but after what he had just seen, everything looked suspicious.

"What time do you call this?"

Chloe's voice hit him like a dart thrown into his back.

"Babe." Toby clutched his chest before spinning around and sweeping her into a hug. "You scared me."

"I scared *you*?" Chloe snapped, pushing him away. "How do you think I felt, waiting for you this late into the night? I called the Highbury and everything, they said you left to walk home ages ago. With your phone off and everything, what was I meant to think?!"

"Sorry. Sorry, babe." He rubbed his eyes. "I didn't turn it off, the battery died."

"And the rest?!"

"Look, just . . . I don't know. I don't know how to describe it," he muttered, glancing back towards the window.

"Something weird happened. Very weird, full-strength weird. I

186

saw something over by the Torrens, I can't figure it out, but it was definitely . . . off."

"Whatever." Chloe rolled her eyes. "I'm going to bed, now that I know you're still alive."

Toby nodded, knowing that there would be no benefit to arguing with her. The bedroom door slammed shut and he collapsed onto the couch. It wasn't until he pulled his shoes off that he saw the dirt and mud splashed all over him. Hoping a shower would settle his mind, he dragged himself towards the bathroom.

If anything, the water woke him up, every drop pelting him with images of black SUVs and oozing green slime. The images clawed at his brain, and he knew that sleep wasn't on the cards for him yet. After drying himself off, he sat down at the kitchen table with a sheet of paper and a pen. He still had no idea what he'd seen, but he wanted to make sure he remembered every detail.

"What are you doing?" Chloe stared down at him.

Toby blinked through hazy vision and noticed sunlight streaming through the window. He didn't remember falling asleep, but could feel the red marks that the surface of the table had left on his face.

"What is that?" Chloe frowned as she crossed the room. "Did you stay up all night . . . drawing?"

Toby rubbed his face as he straightened up. Vague and groggy, he attempted to sort the papers that were spread out in front of him.

"Here. Come look." He gestured with both hands. "This is what I saw last night. This is the reason it took me so long to walk home."

Chloe narrowed her eyes as she peered down at the mess of papers.

"There was this green stuff, all oozing through the river." Toby shuffled through handwritten scribbles that bordered on illegible. "These guys, these secret agent looking guys, they turned up in a black SUV and sprayed it all with foam."

"Toby." Chloe placed a hand on his shoulder. "Are you . . . okay?"

"Yeah, fine," Toby muttered. "I managed to hide, so they didn't see me."

"That's not what I meant, babe."

Toby's eyes were sore, and he was dizzy from lack of sleep, but he picked himself up to look square at Chloe. "I know this sounds crazy," he ranted. "But you know I'm telling the truth right now. Surely you do."

"I can see that you think you're telling the truth." She looked him up and down, shaking her head with visible concern. "Are you sure you're okay? This is weird, babe."

188

"I know. It's weird. It is." Toby rubbed his eyes again. "I don't know how to explain it, I don't know what it was. But that's what I saw."

Chloe stared at him for a moment longer before pulling him into a hug. She stroked the back of his head, a loving gesture to soothe her frazzled boyfriend. "Maybe you should take the night off work," she spoke in a gentle tone. "You need to get some rest. Sleep. Take care of yourself."

"Would do me good, for sure." Toby stood up and stretched his legs. "But I can't, not today. We're already short-staffed, and there's footy on."

Chloe shook her head, keeping a close eye on Toby as he tripped over his feet. "Well that's your decision, then, isn't it?" She sighed. "Just, please take care of yourself. I worry about you sometimes."

Toby nodded, failing to stifle a yawn. His mind was full of muffled chaos, leaving him without anything coherent to say. In place of words, he settled for a tight hug and a kiss on the forehead. Chloe kissed him back before picking up her bag and walking out the door. As Toby heard the ute's engine start, he turned over his notes so he couldn't see them.

* * *

Toby hated spending a bus fare for such a short ride, but the idea of walking to work had never been so unappealing. He was still red-eyed and bleary from lack of sleep, and pulled his hood over his eyes as the bus lurched past Linear Park. When he slunk through the doors of the Highbury Hotel, it was the first time in months that he hadn't been humming his signature tune.

"Hey, there's the bastard." Alex smirked. "Get up to no good last night, did you?"

"What?" Toby frowned.

"Your missus called after you left." Alex winked. "She didn't sound thrilled, mate."

"Ah. Right. Yeah," Toby grumbled. "Yeah, nah, it's all good. Just walked the long way home and my phone died. She got worried."

"Sure thing," Alex laughed. "Whatever you reckon."

Toby was in no mood to play along with Alex's light-hearted banter. He grabbed an apron and a dish cloth, checking his phone before he put it away. When he saw a message from Chloe, he opened it as fast as he could.

Here . . . this would explain what you saw last night! There's always a logical explanation xoxo

Toby clicked the link, immediately recognising the location from the preview image.

"What's up?" Alex craned his neck to see over Toby's shoulder.

"Algae, by the looks." Toby frowned. "In the reservoir at Hope Valley. They're calling it an outbreak." He skimmed the rest of the article, his eyes bouncing over descriptions that sounded wrong in a way he couldn't articulate.

"Algae," Alex scoffed. "Fascinating stuff. Another missing person reported this morning, and you're keeping up to date with the latest in moss and plants. Glad you don't write the news."

"You don't write the news, you report the news. You're not supposed to make it up," Toby snapped, shoving the phone back into his pocket. "Wait—another missing person? What, locally?"

"Very." Alex nodded. His grin vanished as the words left his mouth, and he wiped his face to cover the change in demeanour. "Last seen near the picnic area at Hope Valley. Chilling stuff, if you ask me."

"Yeah, okay. Shit." Toby shuddered.

"Yeah," Alex repeated, his expression growing more sombre with every word. "Gotta say, I swear I recognised him from the picture. Must be good odds that he's had a drink here at some point."

Toby turned his attention to wiping down an already spotless counter. Threads of various thoughts dangled next to each other in his head, but weren't quite connecting. Something was bothering him on a deep level, and he couldn't quite attribute it to the news alone. When he saw a familiar face approaching the bar, he jumped at the chance to distract himself.

"Jimmy." He clapped his hands. "Warm out there, is it?"

"Yeah, just a bit." Jimmy wiped the sweat off his brow, pouring himself a glass of water from the jug at the end of the bar. "Decided to get a bit of exercise, for a change. Forgot how bloody steep some of these streets are."

"You're not wrong," Toby whistled. "Pint of pale should fix you up, yeah?"

"My thoughts exactly." Jimmy grinned. He downed the water in a single gulp before sliding the glass back to Toby.

"Might be a good game tonight." Toby breezed through his standard small talk as he swapped pint for payment.

"Might be." Jimmy shrugged. "That would all depend on whether you support-"

In an instant, the man froze. His beer dropped to the floor, the plastic glass spinning in a puddle of foam. Toby stood, watching in helpless shock as Jimmy's eyes bulged, green veins splitting through his pupils. A sickening gurgle escaped his throat before he collapsed.

"Call triple zero," Alex barked, rushing to Jimmy's side. "Now!"

With shaking hands, Toby grabbed for the phone next to the register. His vision was spinning from the sight of Jimmy's swollen veins. As he called for the ambulance, his voice sounded foreign and muddled in his own ears. His focus was trapped on the green tinge of Jimmy's veins, and the frozen expression on his face. Trying to find anything that could help him look away, he grabbed for the plastic water glass on the counter. Still talking to the emergency services operator, he watched as a green substance spread through a crack in the plastic. Without pausing to think about it, he plucked the glass from the counter, wrapped it in a towel, and slid it into his bag.

* * *

"Oh my God, babe." Chloe pulled Toby into a hug as soon as he walked through the door. "Are you OK? Have you heard any more about what happened?"

Toby let himself be comforted for a moment while he composed himself, running through the words in his head before he said them out loud.

"The ambos got there pretty quick, but it was already too late," he sighed. "Whatever killed him, it killed him fast."

"Probably a heart attack." Chloe led Toby to the couch. "Seems like the most likely cause to me."

"Nah." Toby ruffled up his hair. "Nah, they said it didn't look like that. It was weird. He went all . . . green."

"Try not to think about it," Chloe replied. She kept one hand on his shoulder, reaching for the remote control with the other. The TV flickered into life to reveal a screen full of names and faces. They varied in ages, genders, and settings, but there was one that captured Toby's attention in an instant. It was the woman from the other day's news report, presented in the same smiling picture. From there, he didn't need the captions to know that all those other faces belonged to people that had met the same fate, whatever that fate might have been. Without saying a word, Chloe changed the channel. The screen switched to a pop culture round-up, featuring grainy footage of an old kids' gameshow. A minor celebrity laughed as he described the experience of being covered with bright, green slime for the benefit of family entertainment.

"Oh. Wait." Toby sat up and reached for his bag. "There was something I noticed."

Chloe watched in silence as Toby dug through crumpled papers and loose change. It wasn't long before he found the plastic glass, still contained in the folds of a dish towel. He unwrapped it one small piece at a time, as if he were pulling away a mummy's bandages.

"Toby," Chloe piped up. "What are you—"

She stopped mid-sentence when she saw the glass. The green substance had been little more than a speck when Toby first spotted it, but since then, it had spread. A little slimy blob wavered back and forth inside the plastic, growing before their eyes. Toby yelped at the sight of it, but kept the glass in his hand and pulled a lighter from his pocket. Thinking fast, he torched the crack that had allowed the green ooze to slip inside

194

the pane, melting it shut. As the plastic burned and blistered, the slime shrunk away from the heat and stopped moving. With a shaking hand, Toby placed it down onto the coffee table.

"Jimmy drank from that," he declared. "Water, a big old gulp of it. His veins went just that shade of green, I knew there was something not right about it."

Chloe gripped the arm of the couch, her mouth hanging open. She looked pale and sick as she stared at the plastic glass, shaking her head without saying a word.

"This is it, I guarantee you." Toby jumped to his feet. "This is the stuff I saw at Linear Park. Bet it's the stuff in Hope Valley as well. Algae, my arse."

"You don't—you don't think—" Chloe's voice wavered. "You don't think this has anything to do with those missing people, do you?"

Toby turned around to look at her. He didn't say anything, but he could feel the expression on his own face, and he knew what it was telling her. Chloe cast her eyes to the floor, holding one hand over her mouth. Toby took a deep breath and picked up his bag.

"Whatever this is." He straightened his back. "I'm going to figure it out."

"Babe." Chloe jumped up beside him. "Are you sure about this?"

"Yeah. I am." Toby nodded. "Someone's gotta do it. Better me than someone who doesn't give a shit."

Chloe gripped Toby's shoulders, looking him square in the eye. After a moment of contemplation, she sighed, kissed him, and turned her attention back to the green substance in the plastic glass. "OK," she conceded. "I'm going to take a closer look at this. Please be safe. And please, keep your phone turned on."

Toby nodded again, tightened the straps on his bag, and walked out the door.

* * *

Toby measured his pace in careful steps as he walked along the Torrens. Moving too fast held the risk of missing something crucial, but he also didn't want to take too long. He checked his phone to make sure it still had plenty of charge, and noted the time in the process.

"Hmm," he vocalised. The sound echoed through the trees and over the river, breaking the overwhelming quiet. Hearing the way a single syllable bounced back to his own ears, Toby realised what was making him so uncomfortable. The trail wasn't just quiet, it was completely silent. There was neither human nor animal to be heard, no birdsong, no buzzing insects, not even a scratching scurry of the critters that hid in the bushes.

For some reason, this observation was more terrifying than any other that Toby had made so far. He picked up his pace and ran, puffing and panting until he arrived at Lower North-East Road.

"Come on," he urged himself. "Figure it out. Do something."

His mind continued to spin as he walked up the hill to the Hope Valley Reservoir fence. This was the spot where he usually paused to appreciate the view, but tonight, it was blocked by a tall, plastic barrier.

"Hope Valley Reservoir Reserve is closed until further notice due to algae outbreak," Toby read aloud. "We apologise for any inconvenience."

He took a step back to assess the barrier. It was tall enough to block the view, but didn't look like it would be too hard to scale. "Come on, come on," Toby muttered to himself. "Now or never. Do it."

Fixing his sight on the top of the barrier, he took a running leap and pulled himself over the top.

He had seen the drop behind the fence enough times to be ready for it. Still, his landing was far from elegant, and sent him rolling into scratchy bark and twigs. When he looked up, he forgot all about his bruises. The entire reservoir was bubbling green, oozing up onto the banks. On the other side, the dam wall was cracking under slime that looked heavy enough to hammer away at it with every gust of wind.

"Right. Okay," Toby muttered under his breath. "That's not ideal." Creeping around the reservoir's edge, he stayed as close to the fence as he could. He kept his eyes on the slime, looking away only to watch where he was putting his feet. It didn't take him long to observe that the pulsating green ooze was moving without any visible force being applied to it. The wind blew one way, and the slime pushed back against it, green tendrils slapping like whips onto nearby trees.

Toby jumped backwards when a stray splash of green was flung in his direction. It threw him off balance, and he stumbled into a pile of branches that snapped under his feet. In an instant, the entire reservoir went still.

Toby's mind raced as he stared at the thick, green substance that had suddenly frozen in place. The slime was positioned in awkward shapes, heaped into piles and towers that couldn't have occurred by any natural process. Before Toby could even begin to figure out what was going on, every single shape lurched in his direction. This was followed by a second lurch, and then a third, until it became obvious that the entire reservoir was aware of his presence. Without stopping to think, Toby turned on his heel and ran.

Hope Valley Reservoir Reserve had been surrounded on all sides by the same plastic barriers, blocking every fence and gate. Reminding himself that he had already cleared the barrier once, Toby picked a spot and powered towards it.

Behind him, the slime squelched along the path and crunched branches in its wake. When he was close enough, he held his breath and jumped, managing to grip the plastic with aching fingers.

"Come on, you bastard," he hissed at himself. Red-faced and covered in dirt, he pulled himself all the way up and tumbled into a heap on the other side. He rolled over, fighting to catch his breath, and saw a green waterfall cascade over the barrier. Not wasting a second, Toby picked himself up and sprinted towards the road.

"Toby!"

The voice hit him like a hammer as he recognised it.

"Chloe?!" he gasped. "What the hell are you doing here?! It's dangerous!"

"No shit!" she snapped. "That's why I came!" She tugged on his arm, shoving him aside as a piece of the reservoir fence clattered to the ground where he'd been standing.

As he caught his breath, Toby realised that Chloe was setting up a hose with the biggest nozzle he'd ever seen. "Chloe!" He watched her run to attach the hose to something in the back of the ute. "Chloe, what the hell?!"

"I watched the green stuff in that cup," she yelled as she adjusted the nozzle. "It was right inside the plastic, but it died after it was sealed up. Kept growing until it filled the space and suffocated itself."

Toby stepped back, still clueless as to what Chloe was doing.

"If we can trap it in a secure enough space, it'll do the same, no matter how much of it there is." Chloe shouted. "We just have to make sure it's contained, with no way to seep out."

"And how do we do that?!" Toby yelled back.

"This is that spray-on rubber. The one we were using for waterproofing at work," she explained, still adjusting the nozzle. "I don't know if it's going to work, but it might."

Toby heard a click as Chloe made her final adjustment. With the aid of a sharp push from his girlfriend, he stumbled out of the way to let her lunge forward. A massive blast of black liquid exploded into the air, colliding with the slime as it flew up towards it. When the rubber started sticking, the slime pummelled harder against it. In a giant wave, the entirety of the green ooze lurched away from the reservoir to climb over the barrier. Piece by piece, it pulled itself together to defend against Chloe's attack.

"It's trying to fight." Toby could only stare. "It knows what it's doing."

"And it's shooting itself in the foot!" Chloe hollered. "Look!"

Doing his best to stay out of Chloe's way, Toby watched as the entirety of the slime oozed into one singular entity.

"It thinks that's gonna make it stronger." Toby's eyes bulged at the sight of it.

"And it's making this easier for me," Chloe cackled. "It can think, but it's not that smart!"

"I know the type!" Toby cheered back.

With all the green ooze pouring into one spot, Chloe was able to coat its surface in liquid rubber. The black spray stuck to the slime in a way it couldn't seem to escape. The rubber blistered on contact, which only made the slime fight back harder. It swung back and forth in desperate motions, allowing Chloe to hit it from every angle. Gradually, it shrunk and slowed until it fell to the ground, trapped in a heap by the rubber.

Jerking the hose along behind her, Chloe ran forward. She sprayed every inch of green, making sure that there was no gap that could allow the slime to escape. Even after the massive, gurgling pile had stopped moving, she sprayed until her tank was empty.

Encased in rubber, the slime pulsated, a crackling, electric fizz jolting against its prison. Its fight ended with a horrible bubbling wail, before it all fell silent. Chloe dropped the hose and fell to her knees, laughing like a maniac. Toby ran over and threw his arms around her, laughing along with her.

"Good job, babe." He thumped her on the back. "Absolutely nailed it."

"Yeah, thanks," she cackled. "Someone had to do it, right?"

He pulled her close and kissed her, taking time to enjoy the moment before they both climbed to their feet. Together, they stared at the silent, black lump on the ground in front of them. It remained motionless, but Toby and Chloe stood there until sirens began to sound in the distance.

"Sounds like our cue to head out." Toby looked over his shoulder towards the ute. "Hey, how much of that rubber stuff did you have? I'm amazed it all fit in the tray."

"Yeah." Chloe laughed again. "Some, uh, adjustments were required. We might be catching the bus for a while."

As fire engines careened towards the reservoir gates, Toby and Chloe walked back down the hill to Paradise.

About the Author:

Sarah Jane Justice is a speculative fiction author living on Gaurna Land. Her short stories have been published by Eerie River Publishing, Black Beacon Books, and Dark Dossier Magazine, as well as being brought to life in episodes of Hawk & Cleaver's horror podcast 'The Other Stories'. She is also a highly acclaimed spoken word artist, musician, and poet.

A stone's throw from the haunted Rundle Mall is the South Australian Museum, home to more bodies than the average cemetery.

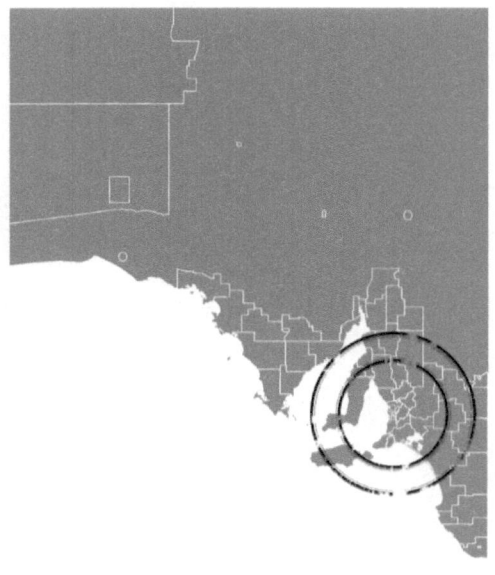

CRATE 986

Chris Mason

Ellie met her father at the side entrance to the museum. He unlocked the door, checked no one else was hanging around in the alleyway, and let her in. They crossed the room where the large exotic mammals were displayed: apes, bears, big cats, an elephant. The exhibits were forlorn without the daytime crowds, and the taxidermy was showing its age. At the lift, Arnold Bower punched the down button. Ellie knew then he was taking her to the biological science research collection housed in the museum's lower ground floors.

From the lift, Ellie followed him down a corridor, past steel cabinets and freezer units. She'd been here many times before. The rooms to either side contained cupboards and shelves crammed with fauna: birds, reptiles, mammals, marine life, insects and amphibians, all preserved in various forms. Most of the specimens were contained in ethanol filled jars, everything from dingo heads to tiny lizards. Cured pelts of mammals hung in cupboards, the smell of camphor wafting off them; shallow drawers held bones—all meticulously numbered and nested in tissue paper. Jammed into every conceivable space were filing cabinets loaded with boxes of invertebrate exoskeletons, dried and stabbed with pins. Glass-doored fridges held tissue specimens and freezers overflowed with recent roadkill. The public liked to contribute to the assembly of dead.

For most of Ellie's childhood, the labyrinth beneath the South Australian Museum of Natural History had been her backyard, on account of Arnold holding the most senior position within the research department. Instead of spending weekends at the pool or on a netball court, she'd rollerbladed through the vast underground complex exploring every corner in the place. By the time Ellie finished university she was so used to being around dead things, it didn't bother her anymore. She wasn't a fan of the room with the jars of parasites, coiled tapeworms and the like. They made her squeamish. She'd rather not know about anything that could reside in a stomach or burrow under the skin. But as hideous as they were, they didn't frighten her. Which was why, racing to keep up with her father, Ellie wondered what on earth all the fuss was about. What was so important he'd asked her to meet at the museum in the middle of the night? And why was he so nervous? The man was sweating buckets.

They entered a stairwell and descended another floor. At the bottom Arnold swiped a security card and opened the door to the underground loading dock. He was out of breath.

"Has something new arrived?" Ellie asked, breaking their silence.

Arnold shook his head.

"Then what?"

"Something is going out."

"At this time of night?" There was nothing unusual about sending out parts of the collection to other museums. It happened all the time. So why all the secrecy?

"I want you to see it before it goes," said Arnold.

Ellie frowned. Was there something in the collection she hadn't seen? She didn't think so. All through university, she'd done volunteer work at the research centre. Anything she'd missed growing up she was soon privy to, mainly because she'd been assigned to implementing the new barcoding system. The job was slow and tedious, but after four years of adding records into the computer, Ellie knew where every bone and body part was stored. Or thought she did.

Together they crossed the vast concrete bunker. At the far end was a sliding steel gate, large enough for a truck to get through. Beyond the gate was a ramp that spiralled up and out of the museum building to the western exit. Before he reached the gate, Arnold veered off between stacks of packing crates piled in front of a roller door. He keyed in a code and the door rattled opened. Inside was a shipping container.

"Okay, I never knew about this," said Ellie, curious.

"No one does." Arnold checked his watch. "We've got a little over two hours before they get here."

"Who?" asked Ellie.

"You have to promise me not to tell another soul."

"Of course."

Arnold rubbed his brow. "Two officials from the Pentagon."

"The Pentagon?" Ellie studied her father's face. He looked ill, his ruddy complexion now pale as soap. "Are you serious?"

"It'll make more sense once I open this up." He unlocked the container and pulled back a tarp to reveal a crate. It took up most of the space and was anchored by thick ropes tied to metal rings welded to the walls. Stencilled on the front of the crate were the numbers 986.

Ellie raised an eyebrow. "How long has this been here?"

"A while."

"I'm guessing the crate isn't empty."

"It's not," said Arnold.

"None of the specimens are supposed to be held down here, not in the transit area. Who else knows about it?"

"Just me . . . and now you." He gave her a weak smile. "As far as I know, my predecessor was the only other person who knew about the delivery, and clearly his idea to hide the container in plain sight worked. In the forty years I've been in this place, not one person has ever asked me what was behind the roller doors. Not even you."

"Sorry I let you down." Ellie returned his smile. "I assumed it was full of old packing boxes. It's a cardboard graveyard down here."

"What's the golden rule?"

Ellie groaned. "Yeah, I know. Never assume."

His smile broadened for a second then winked out. "Are you ready?"

"I suppose so." Ellie had no idea what was in the crate. A shiver ran the length of her spine, and what should have been excitement started to feel a lot more like dread. Did she really want to know what her father had kept hidden from her all these years? The man was a scientist, it was not in his DNA to bury a research opportunity–much less conceal a body unless he had a very good reason.

Arnold slid back a series of bolts and the front of the crate popped open. Secured within a framework of timber was a giant glass tank. He handed her a torch. "Get up inside, so you can have a good look."

Ellie stepped into the container and up to the crate. It was twice as tall as she was. She shone a beam of light into the tank. A dark mass floated in it. Her eyes widened. Whatever the creature was, it was huge. Ellie stepped closer. She took in the thick matt of black hair, the high forehead and hairless face, the wide flat nose, the puckered mouth showing an incisor the length of her arm. Where the neck should have been was a tangle of ragged skin. Her breath caught in her throat. The tank held the severed head of a giant ape.

Ellie stared at her father in disbelief. "Is that what I think it is?"

"A cryptid?"

"A bloody gorilla!"

"It is."

She didn't know what shocked her more. The sight of the impossible thing, or her father's acceptance of it.

"They don't grow to this size. Ever," said Ellie, her voice tiny.

"Tell that to old Winston here," said Arnold.

Ellie couldn't take her eyes away from the magnificent beast. There was something sorrowful about the face despite its terrifying proportions. She rested her head against the glass. For a moment she wondered what it would have been like to be this close when it was alive. Feeling its hot breath on her body, hearing the beat of its heart, looking into its eyes, brown and deep, and seeing her fear reflected there. "You call him Winston?"

Arnold shrugged. "I thought it suited him."

"Where did he come from?"

"Originally? An island off Indonesia, I believe. We acquired him through the Smithsonian."

Her jaw dropped. "The Smithsonian? Do they have the rest of him?"

"I couldn't say, but I doubt it."

Ellie's mind struggled with the improbability of the situation. "How is it that the scientific community doesn't know about this? How does the entire *world* not know about this?"

"It's been a well-guarded secret. Think of the implications if word got out a real King Kong had been found. It'd be open season on every island between here and China."

"How does Merian C. Cooper figure into the equation?"

"He doesn't. The man had a great imagination though, I'll give him that. In a way he did Winston here a favour. Cooper created a monster so believable, the truth got lost in it. A lot of legends are like that."

"If you tell me you have Bigfoot down here as well, I'll scream."

Arnold laughed and it was good to see his mood brighten.

"Aside from the fact I'm looking at the remains of one freaking ginormous animal, what's hardest to get my head around is why the Smithsonian would part with something so incredibly important."

"They didn't have a choice. During the cold war they had to move him to keep him safe."

"And they chose Adelaide?"

"Few people could stick a pin in a map to say where we are."

"You may have a point, Dad," Ellie agreed. "When did the museum get him?"

"Nineteen sixty-one. Stanley passed the secret on to me when he retired."

"In all that time, did the Smithsonian keep in contact with either you or Stanley?"

"No, not a word. To be honest, I thought my friend here had been forgotten. Then out of the blue, I get a phone call."

"From the Pentagon." Ellie thought on this for a while. "I understand the whole high security aspect, but it doesn't feel right. Why would the military want to get their hands on a giant gorilla?"

Arnold took off his glasses, wiped them, and placed them back on the tip of his nose. "That's the bit that worries me too."

"Where do you think they'll take him?"

"At a guess, Pine Gap. After that, no idea."

"Has anyone from our government spoken to you?"

"No."

"Do you think they know what's going on?"

"I'd like to think so. But then why didn't someone from our end, pick up a phone and talk to me?"

"And you're sure the person you spoke to is who they say they are?"

"Oh, yes. They knew too many details. The crate number, for instance. The date Winston arrived. Some things about Stanley. Plus, I googled the man I spoke to and couldn't find a thing about him. A sure sign he's legit."

Ellie gave him a nudge. "Look at you, my father the master spy."

She returned her attention to the creature in the tank. The task of preserving the animal would have been precarious. "If the head has been fixed with formalin, the DNA will be damaged," she considered. "He's in an ethanol mix?"

"One hundred percent pure ethanol. I tested it."

"Bloody hell, they didn't skimp on the alcohol when they filled the tank. How did you get access?"

"There's a small hatch up top. It's enough to get a hand through."

"Have you taken any other samples?"

"Some hair and skin tissue from the scalp. And you're right, he hasn't been fixed with formalin. The DNA is still retrievable. Whoever preserved him did a good job."

Ellie sighed. "I can't believe you kept this to yourself. Did Mum know?"

"Your mother never could keep a secret. I loved her, but how she liked to talk. So, no, I never told her."

"And you think I *can* keep a secret?"

"I'm counting on it. Although it makes no difference now. By tomorrow morning Winston will be gone, and no one will be any the wiser."

"I get the feeling you're going to miss him."

"I will. I often come down here with a coffee and sit and talk to the old boy, after everyone has clocked off."

"Talk about what?"

"Life. You know, the ups and downs of the everyday. How the world has changed . . . and how it hasn't."

This surprised Ellie. Her father wasn't much of a conversationalist. When he did have something to say, it was more often than not about work.

"I also chat a lot about you."

"Me?"

"Why not? Winston knows all the stories. He knows about the day you fell off the swing at school and broke your arm. How we both cried at the airport when you left to go study in Japan for a year. I read him the emails you sent while you were away. I told him about your wedding and how beautiful you looked. He knows about the little farmhouse you bought with Ava and all the rescue animals you've taken in. I even told him about your stubborn streak and how I let you win every argument we have."

Ellie laughed. "Is that right, Dad? I never knew you were so generous . . . or sentimental."

"Winston has taught me a lot. Learned some things about myself too. The least I could do in return was give him some company while he was down here in the dark."

Ellie stepped up to the tank again and ran her hand down the glass. Once, this creature had been an apex predator. But no more. A thought niggled at her. "The US wouldn't try to weaponize him, would they? Clone him, or do a Frankenstein number with the head, somehow?"

Arnold shrugged. "I'd like to say it couldn't be done, but . . ."

Ellie paced the length of the crate and back again. "He's been resting here for decades, why can't they leave him be?"

Arnold didn't answer.

"It doesn't matter how big or fierce an animal is, humans will fuck them over. Every. Single. Time." Ellie folded her arms across her chest. She had a fire in her belly. "Well, I say they can't have him. He shouldn't have been taken in the first place."

"Ellie, I understand, but I'm afraid there is nothing to be done," said Arnold.

"You didn't raise me to be a quitter, Dad. You're not one either."

"The two of us can't go up against the US military!"

"Why not? What can they do? I mean, c'mon. At the end of the day, they're a bureaucracy like any other. Their wheels turn slowly, let's take advantage of that."

"I could lose my job."

"How? The board loves you, and who's going to kick up a stink if nobody else around here knows about this crate except you and Stanley–and he's been dead thirty years? Here's a thought. Maybe Stanley never told you a damn thing. Maybe the crate disappeared on his watch. Was there ever any paperwork?"

"No. It was only ever word of mouth."

"So, how can anyone point a finger at you? All you have to do is put on your stuffy professor act and tell them, you're very sorry, but there's no computer record for a crate nine eight six. Our barcoding system is second to none, and *nothing* slips through the cracks here. But of course, if they want to go through every one of the five million archive records we've got stored somewhere, that's fine. They will, however, need to go through formal protocols first."

"What you're saying is bury them in admin."

Ellie grinned. "It works for everything else around here. I'm still trying to chase a research grant I lodged three years ago."

By the look on Arnold's face, Ellie knew he was entertaining the idea. He skipped ahead to the logistics. "Hypothetically then, if we do decide to give the middle finger to the most powerful nation on earth, how do you suggest we move Winston?"

Ellie tapped a finger on her lips. "How much does the crate weigh?"

"A lot. Let's see if we can figure it out. A silverback weighs around two hundred and twenty kilos, correct?"

"Yes." Working in a zoo for the better part of a decade, Ellie knew her primates.

Arnold stood back, hands on hips. "The movie monster version was about eighteen times the size of a male gorilla. Winston would be around that mark."

"We only have his head to consider, so let's keep it simple and say it weighs about a third of the body mass." Ellie did a mental calculation.

"Don't forget to factor in the Ethanol."

"Ethanol weighs less than water. How many litres do you think he's swimming in?"

They settled on a maximum weight of four tonnes for the crate and its contents.

"We need a truck with a crane," said Ellie.

"Hang on." Arnold pulled his phone out and punched in a number. It rang out and he called again. "Hi Griff. The whale carcass you brought in last week, how much did it weigh?" There was a pause. "Yeah, I know it's the middle of the night." He waited then held a thumb up. "Twelve tonne, heh."

Ellie punched the air. Too easy.

"I know I'm stretching the friendship, but how soon can you get your truck over to the museum?" Arnold nodded and hung up. "He'll be here in forty minutes."

Ellie checked her watch. "Cutting it a bit fine, but it should work."

Beads of sweat dotted Arnold's receding hairline. "All we have to do now is figure out where the hell we are going to put him."

Ellie tapped her forehead. "Up here for thinking, down there for dancing." She shuffled her feet. The ideal location had already come to her.

* * *

Thirty kilometres north of Adelaide was the museum's second research facility. The huge warehouses at Dry Creek housed tanks of water kept at body temperature, their sole purpose to strip the meat off the bone. Other tanks held colonies of slaters or dermestids that provided a similar service. Ellie was eight when her father had taken her out for her first visit. Observing life forms decomposing wasn't for everybody and the smell took a while to get used to. Although she'd gagged at the whales rotting in the water tanks, Ellie's fascination held. She still took the occasional trip out there when she could.

Griff Anders provided transport for the Dry Creek operations and was used to putting all sorts of strange things on the back of his truck. Ellie liked him. He was one of the good guys, got on with the job, and didn't ask questions. For his efforts, all he requested was that the standard after-hours fee of two cartons of pale ale be upped to three, given the early callout. Ellie had a request of her own—Griff put his cigarette out. They didn't need his nicotine addiction anywhere near a tank with a few thousand litres of ethanol in it.

They got the crate onto the back of the truck and out of the museum basement with fifteen minutes to spare. Security was not an issue. The surveillance camera in the loading area hadn't worked in weeks—God bless funding cutbacks—and the guard on duty at that hour of the morning was on the other side of the complex, doing his rounds in the museum's exhibition halls. Ellie went with Griff. Arnold remained behind, armed with a treasury of weasel words to buy enough time for them to get the precious cargo as far away from the Pentagon goons as possible.

On the South Eastern freeway, Griff's truck joined the other overnight long-haulers. The journey was slow. On the way, Ellie got her phone out. The call she made involved a delicate negotiation. More personal than business. There was a lot at stake, and she couldn't afford to stuff it up.

The truck reached the Monarto Zoological Park an hour before dawn. Ava, the head keeper at the park, met them at the western entrance. She was driving a backhoe. As soon as they entered through the gates, the chimpanzees in the primate enclosure started screaming. Lions paced their perimeter fence, their roars booming over 15000 hectares of safari park. Kangaroos bounded across the top paddocks, galahs shrieked, and the southern white rhino stamped its feet as they passed. Ellie shuddered. Somehow, the animals knew. One of their own was coming home.

In a large patch of dense scrub on the far side of the park, away from the tourist centre and viewing trails, Ava used the backhoe to scoop out a hole big enough to bury Winston. Ellie admired the way Ava got things done. No fuss, no dithering, no problem with making big decisions on the fly. She was smart and practical. Ellie would trust Ava with her life. That's why she'd married her.

When Ava was done, Griff used the crane on the back of his truck to lower the crate into the grave.

"Thanks Griff. You are a legend," said Ellie. "We owe you one."

"No problem. Your dad has done more than a few favours for me over the years."

"And if anyone grills you?"

"I delivered roadkill the museum didn't have use for. Couple of big roos, couple of wombats. Frozen treats for the big cats."

Ellie grinned. "Love your work, Griff."

After Griff was gone, Ava rounded on Ellie. "Now tell me what you wouldn't say over the phone. What's in the crate?"

"If I said it was something from the large mammal collection, would you believe me?"

"No."

"Why?"

"It makes no sense. Museums aren't in the habit of dumping their research specimens or their exhibits."

Ellie blew air through her lips. "How about this then. Remember when the Capri theatre was screening some of the old classics last year? We went and saw that black and white version of King Kong?"

"What the hell has that got to do with anything?"

"Humour me."

"Alright, I'll give you a free pass." Ava narrowed her eyes, thinking. "The theatre had a man playing the Wurlitzer organ. It was your idea of a romantic night out."

"That's it. You teared up all the way through the movie."

"It was sad. Of course, I cried. And I don't care if it is all make-believe, no creature deserves to be treated like that."

"You love your primates."

"I love all animals. It's why we do what we do, isn't it?"

Ellie smiled. She knew how much Ava loved this park and would never leave—despite the long hours and the constant fight for funding. She was making a difference here. She'd worked hard to make a good home for the animals.

Ellie put her arms around Ava and kissed her . "Love you."

"You're not going to tell me what's in the crate, are you?"

"Let's just say, he's someone special."

"Nothing the palaeontologists will kick up a stink over?"

"No dinosaur bones, I promise," said Ellie.

"Damn, I wanted it to be a monster lizard," Ava joked.

Ellie licked her lips. "You got me, I stuffed Godzilla in a box." She paused. "You can take a look if you want to."

"No, it's okay. As long as it's not a shipment of drugs . . . or human remains, I'm good." She smiled at Ellie and climbed back up into the backhoe.

Ellie stood at the edge of the hole, looking on as soil covered the crate. "Rest easy, big guy," she whispered. The earth beneath her feet rumbled. For a brief moment she thought she heard a grunt, felt something sniff her face. A warm breath lifted her hair and then it was gone.

In the east the sun peeked above the flat horizon. A flock of corellas took flight. The lions paced the fence, and the giraffes and zebras grazed their pretend African plains. Behind a wall of glass, meerkats stood watch. In the primate enclosure, every chimpanzee bowed their head in silence, a tribute to the king resting among them.

222

Meanwhile, seventy kilometres away, Arnold handed a pen to a man in uniform, and watched him fill out an archive request form.

About the Author:

Chris Mason is a writer of short stories and novellas. She is a Shirley Jackson award finalist and has won several Aurealis awards and an Australian Shadows award for her work. Chris lives on Peramangk land in the Adelaide Hills of South Australia.
You can visit her at: facebook.com/chrismasonhorrorwriter or on twitter @Chris_A_Mason.

Once an isolated fishing community with dark secrets, Mandurah is now a thriving regional city with dark secrets.

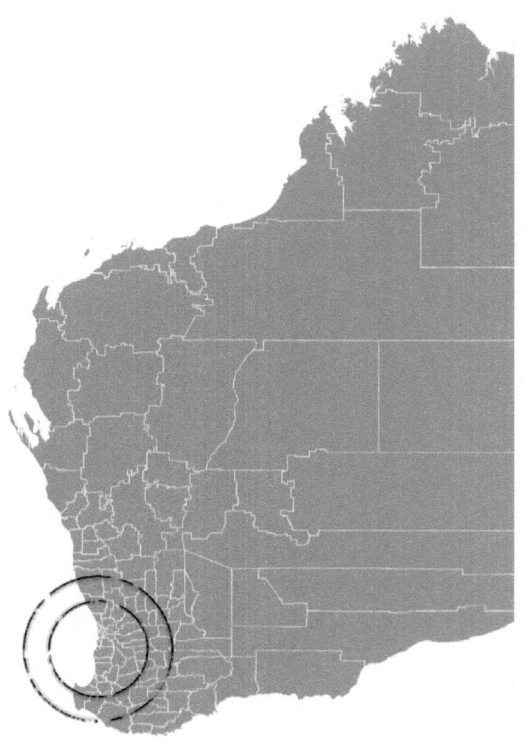

WEATHERING

Emma Louise Gill

Djeran (autumn): the season of adulthood. Cooler weather begins.

There's a toddler floating in the air by your head. Your mouth twitches and you give a tiny wave, then push the soft arms away, towards her mother.

"Incoming," you say.

The woman—you don't remember her name, only that she's a Flyer, too—looks up from her phone in time to catch her child. You try not to judge, but this *is* a Parent's Group. Everyone judges everyone here, from the too-good-to-be-true, two-dad couple to the nanna who reminiscences on 'better times'. Even the group's host has a plastic smile, moulded to fit each week's critics and crises. You turn away before anyone can see the accusation in your face.

Isla is sitting on the mat playing with the shape sorter. She selects a chunky star and with intense concentration tries to push it through a square hole. You let her experiment, give an encouraging hum. She doesn't look at you, but her frustration pulses in scarlet bursts through your Mother-Daughter connection, the invisible line that links your minds as indelibly as your womb's umbilical once linked your bodies. Your unique, paired 'quirk'. You send back a pulse of love and reassurance. Golden, like the light on the morning her father left you—a colour *he* neither gave nor received.

But Isla will never lack for love; you promise her that every day.

"When do you think she'll talk?" Kristen leans in from the right. Her boy, Sean, has the most beautiful blond hair. He's sitting on her lap in her wheelchair, and she's braiding with her expert, Patterner fingers. Twist, fold, twist.

You shrug, hiding tension with the movement. Why do people have to keep asking? "When she feels like she needs to, I expect."

"That's right. Her quirk's Telepathy, like yours, Nessie?"

I nod—close enough—noticing Kristen's pink, manicured nails. How does she get the time?

"Amir's quirk is Mathematics. He doesn't show it yet, but it will come."

The comment comes from Farya. You both turn to her with soothing noises. She says it every week. Of course, she doesn't have to worry about secondary quirks manifesting in Amir, since both she and her partner have Maths as primary. She just needs patience. Meanwhile, Amir sits on the floor sucking his fingers, not caring a whit about his future.

"Must be nice." Kristen sighs. "I was up all night trying to figure out what Sean wanted. His screams broke the mirror in the hall. And now we can't find the cat, either."

"Cat hearing *is* extra sensitive," Farya says. "I'd be surprised if she came back at all."

You glare, pushing back the urge to Transmit your thoughts on that answer, then turn to Kristen. Her perfect eyebrows are frowning at Farya, with hollows darkened by lack of sleep and sympathy. "Don't worry about it," you say. "The cat will come back. Have you tried the neighbours?"

She nods. Sighs. "Oh, yeah. That's a good idea."

You twitch your lips again. Your phone vibrates and you grab for it, saved by the alarm you set this morning. A tip you picked up from a website.

"Oh, look at the time. I have to leave early today," you say. Then, "Isla."

Your daughter looks up. Her thoughts are purple and black, confusion with a swirl of rising anger. The star is still in her hand. You crouch by her side and help her push the shape into the correct place, prompting a laugh. The sound is a tingle of joy, and bright yellow overtakes the darkness. You smile. *"Come on."*

She smiles back at you; at the words you sent telepathically, understanding at a level beyond language. You wrap her in

227

your arms, this bundle of child with her wild, curly, dark hair, and you think about how much the others are missing.

Kristen and Farya share a glance. "See you next week, Nessie," they call. "Bye, Isla."

"See you," you say, hand waving because that's what other people do to say goodbye. Baby hands copy the gesture.

Isla nestles into your chest in her carrier. She's getting heavy but you're not ready to give up this last physical reminder of her babyhood. You leave with a final glance at the room. Just an ordinary hall in the back of a church, plastic chairs and patterned rug laid out in the centre, half a dozen children and their carers playing in the cool April morning. You think of them as your friends, sort of—but a friend is someone who brings coffee when you're feeling sick; a friend is someone you can greet at the door in pyjamas and bed hair and tear-streaked mascara, and you know they won't judge because they've done the same. A friend is irreplaceable, and your friends were left behind when you moved here. Away from *him*.

You shake your head and nuzzle Isla's. It smells of coconut shampoo and the distinctive scent of baby: milk, body oils, washing powder. Innocence. Love. Your heart warms and Isla's connection brightens to orange, mingling with your gold.

The morning sun is nearing midday but the wind is brisk. You walk into it to the foreshore, taking your time. Aware of the body attached to yours, of the heart beating next to your own and the tiny toes in their pink socks and sparkling shoes swinging at your hips. The sky is the pale blue of Djeran season, the Noongar name for autumn, and you think about the gloves you've been knitting—poorly—wishing you'd finished them already.

As you pass the boutique baby shop a dress catches your eye and you almost go in, but it's not a good idea. Centrelink isn't due until next week and you'll regret spending, you know you will. The store assistant in the window is arranging a mannequin and her eyes first light up at the two of you, then move on with barely a flicker. She knows you won't come in, somehow. They always know. You wonder if there's a school for shop assistants. Do they teach how to Read customers? To use quirks for more efficient and lucrative sales?

Could they teach *you* to tune in to others better?

Isla's link gains a thread of purple and grey. Worries. Guilt strikes your chest, a deep and familiar pang. Sometimes you Transmit more than you should, more than you realise. You take a deep breath and focus on dispersing your thoughts.

The footbridge here is white and steep, but the canal beneath is deep green and slow. You watch the water flowing, let your thoughts drift along its current, try to see your emotions without feeling them, without tangling Isla in them, too. They are leaves on the stream. Floating on the water they lose their potency; disappear beneath the bridge. You let them go. Loss. Sadness. Anxiety for the future. Concern for your daughter, wondering when she'll speak, when she'll start asking about her father. The inevitable anger at *him* that hasn't faded with time, despite what everyone said. A deep, leaden fear that no one will ever want you again.

Loneliness.

You hold Isla tight and wonder how you can feel this way with your heart's companion in your arms. She falls asleep while the clouds meander and the sun reaches noon, while you watch the water and wish someone could hear you. The greatest irony of being a Transmitter: no one actually *wants* to know your mind.

* * *

Makuru (winter): the season of fertility. Wettest, coldest, and windiest time of year.

You sit beside the river, making the most of a day without rain. Recreational boats pass by; pelicans sail on the estuary like miniature yachts; buoys flash their red and green lights out on the water. Isla is on the grass behind you, chasing seagulls and throwing scraps of bread. Her giggle is a pulse of golden joy that lets you know where she is without having to follow with your eyes. Which is a good thing, because a dolphin has swum up to the quay and is launching themselves out of the water. A white man takes shape mid-leap, water streaming from him. He lands gracefully, bare feet on stained wood.

You stare—and why not? He's in good shape and it's been a long time since you've seen a naked butt that wasn't Isla's. His scalp is bald, his eyes the grey-blue of shallows in a storm. He catches you watching him, removes a plastic pouch from around his neck where it hangs on a blue string, and shakes out a micro-towel. It barely covers anything, and it's the middle of winter. He grins. You blush.

It's been a long time since a man grinned at you, too.

You turn away. Isla's shrieks at the gulls echo telepathically, and that means she's broadcasting—the piercing cry is reaching more than just the birds. People are staring, wincing, covering their ears.

You run to her. "Hush, baby."

A police officer Blinks in. "Is this your child?"

"Hush. The birds are gone. You scared them." You hold her tight. She scared everyone, but now her own fear has risen. Orange, gold, and blue—threads to soothe. *"Calm, now."*

There's a reason nobody likes Transmitters. Who wants someone else's thoughts projected into their head? Only the advertisers and security companies want to hire you, but being a walking billboard or alarm system isn't glamourous, either. You hug Isla and wish the world would give her a chance.

"Move along now, Miss." The officer is a short woman with crisp lines in her uniform and bird crap on one shoulder. Her eyes are small and beady.

Like a crow, you think, and she frowns before you clamp down on your thoughts all the harder. Don't let them hear. The tightness in your chest is moving to your head, turning scarlet.

"We were just leaving, anyway," you say, and scoop Isla up.

But you're not going to be scared away by anyone, superior quirks or not, so you take your time putting her into the carrier. Clip the clips, and leave without a backward glance. Your departure would have been more satisfying if the police officer had stayed to witness it, but only seagulls remained. Once the screaming stopped, no one paid attention to the two of you. There were other shenanigans to be had at the playground. Even the dolphin man had disappeared.

Well, sod them all.

* * *

Birak (first summer): the season of the young. Dry and hot, with cool sea breezes in the afternoon. Time for fire.

Your mood is dark as you wander into a café, despite the bright sunshine. It's the fog you often feel after another Parent's Group meeting, another opportunity for other people to show off their children and their quirks. You tell yourself you're still going for Isla's sake, and hide negative self-talk under false smiles and silent bitterness. But Isla's skill today was crying so much you had to put up a shield to dampen the volume. You couldn't wait to escape.

The café is decorated in dark greens and golds, its polished wood tables scattered with chain brand menus. Isla is asleep on your chest, curls sweaty on her forehead. You really ought to buy a pram. At two, she shouldn't be carried around anymore. But who cares about 'should' anyway? Your mother's last 'should' was shouted at you the last time you spoke. And even though she was right—goddamn, she was right about *him*—you still can't tell her that to her face. Maybe on the phone. One of these days.

You push the thought away like a cloud and consider the girl behind the counter. Her thick black eyeliner reminds you of teenagehood and freedom. "Skinny latte," you order. Then with a glance at the specials list, "A shot of green as well?"

She winks. So does her tattoo, a jolly fuchsia pig on her arm. "Sure."

Green is for Luck, and it could be good or could be bad, but you're feeling young and reckless all of a sudden and asking yourself, *why not?* You've got the extra three dollars from your new job selling tickets for the local pirate cruise, so why shouldn't you give your life a little shake-up? Monotony belongs to the dead.

You step aside to wait while the next customer orders. You give him a second look, then a third. It's the dolphin guy. The one from that day after Parent's Group back in winter. The one you've been unashamedly looking out for on your walks along the Esplanade these past six months. But while you've seen plenty of dolphins, none turned into him.

He orders an espresso, topped up, in a tiny keep cup featuring an Aboriginal design. You aren't surprised at the eco-friendly choice. It makes you smile. Isla gurgles in her sleep. You look down at her, and when the barista calls your name, you are startled to find that dolphin guy is standing beside you.

He cocks his head as you collect your coffee. "Nessie?"

"Um. Yes?" The paper cup is warm in your hand; you grab it with your other as well, as if the warmth will seep through your veins and kickstart your brain. He is wearing board shorts and a white shirt. Sunglasses balance on the back of his neck. He is completely normal and completely extraordinary at the same time. Your heart races.

"Nice name," he says. Does he remember you?

"Barry," the barista calls.

He reaches past you for the takeaway.

"Same to you," you say. Though you don't mean it. *Barry*?

"You don't mean it," he says. His smile is self-deprecating. "But that's okay." He shrugs. "See you around."

Crap, he heard you. You look at your cup. Is the Luck worth it?

With exaggerated care you place it back on the counter, then follow him out. "Sorry," you say.

He turns; outside, the sun bounces off the water into your eyes. You shade them with one hand while the other shields Isla's sleeping face.

"I didn't mean to be rude," you say. "I'm actually Anessa, and this is Isla. I'm a Transmitter."

"I got that," he says. Sips his espresso. We look at each other.

"I just meant . . . I don't know."

He raises an eyebrow.

Sod it. *"I didn't think of Barry as a dolphin name."* Heat rises in your cheeks. That's it, he'll go now. You made a fool of yourself. Making fun of people's names is not going to make you friends. Idiot.

But he laughs. "What should I be called? Flipper?"

"No." Now your entire head is on fire. Transmitting instead of speaking? Your embarrassment surges, thick and scarlet. Isla stirs.

"It's okay." He finishes his drink and tucks the empty cup into his satchel. It's a plain khaki shoulder bag, at odds with the surfer look, yet it works for him. He grins at you. "You're right, of course. My nickname is Barry; my real name's Marron. But that's too oceany to fit in around here, you know. Barry's more 'average Aussie.'"

235

You manage to nod your head. "Oh." And here you are with your Loch Ness Monster nickname.

He frowns, a small dip of his eyebrows. "You broadcast a lot."

"Oh." You wince and tighten your inner walls. "Sorry." Must have been the strain of holding back at Parent's Group. Normally, you feed the bond with Isla so your quirk doesn't become stifled, but that's all. You can't bear other peoples' faces when you Transmit. The expressions like *his*.

"It's okay," Barry says. He smiles.

You smile.

You realise you're standing goofily on the sidewalk, blocking the way for pedestrians. You step onto the grass. He turns to go, but, "Do you live in Mandurah?" you say, and he stops. Two steps and you've caught up. "I mean, I think I saw you before . . ."

"You did see me before." His glance is amused. He walks along the Esplanade path, a steady pace so you can keep up with your toddler-in-arms. "I'm a transient," he adds, though you don't know what that means.

He looks at you as if he heard your thought. Are some quirks more receptive to Transmission than others? It's not something your mother talked about; not that anyone else would volunteer information, either. Each quirk's 'quirks' are kept a secret, only for those in the know.

"Transient is a scientific term for dolphins—and whales—who travel between locations," Barry says. "There are inshore, river, offshore, resident, migratory, and transient types. I spend time in different places along the coast." His mouth curves in an inviting smile, and your racing pulse returns. "We're hard to pin down. We're quite Empathic as well."

You fiddle with Isla's straps.

He pauses, proving his point with a look. "I pick up on thoughts, feelings, and emotions, whereas you project them." His blue-grey eyes alight on Isla. "Your little one does both, I see."

You laugh in surprise. "What?"

Isla's eyes have opened, their clear brown irises focusing on Barry. She is a rainbow of emotion, with the bright green of excitement the strongest. She kicks her legs and sends you a picture of herself running.

"We're going home soon, baby," you tell her back, but her forehead creases and she laces her thoughts with dark brown.

"No. Run."

"Isla," you tut aloud. She kicks again.

"Mummy talk. Isla run."

"You've got an Aqua quirk in your family, don't you? Let her down if you like," Barry says, and Isla smiles at him.

You frown at the two of them, but you're too intrigued to say no. "Conspirators."

237

Undoing her carrier, you let Isla out. She grabs Barry's tanned leg in a fierce hug, then heads off to chase pigeons. You chuckle, pleased that Isla touched someone other than yourself.

Barry laughs too. The sound rings like bronze bells in your ears.

An early afternoon breeze stirs the air, laden with the scent of salt and seaweed from the estuary mouth. You glance at Barry. What does he mean about Aqua? The only watery thing about you is the Nessie nickname your father gave you, the last thing left of him.

Barry gestures to the low esplanade wall. You sit because he asked; he settles beside you. Tanned, gorgeous, interesting. Facing away from the water.

Your head is spinning; you stare at the grass; the birds; the toddler. "Are you going to be around for a while?"

"I don't know yet," he replies.

You try not to let disappointment escape its containment field. But when you gather courage enough to look at him, his eyes meet yours with a hint of contemplation that warms you more than the sun.

* * *

Bunuru (second summer): season of ripening. Hottest part of the year. Time for coastal living.

You're forced to call it 'casual dating' when cornered by Kristen at the play centre. It's the end of summer and the heat has you tossing back Panadol every day.

"So, what's he do?" She prods and pries.

An image of the dolphin man Transforming heats your cheeks a little. "Barry? He's a . . . fisheries observer," you reply, distracting yourself by watching Isla jump about the ball pit, semi-pleased with your evasive—and quite true—answer.

"Oh, really? Does he have a boat?"

"No, I don't think so. Isla!" You pivot. *Tell him to stop if you don't want more balls Teleported at your face.*

"I suppose he has one at work, then."

The other child, a bully in the making, shrieks, hands over his ears.

"Not like that!" "Sorry, just a sec." You wave Kristen off and almost trip over in your hurry to Isla. She grins, unrepentant, and for a moment you wish you could praise her. Instead, you put on your Mum Face and frown. "No death threats in the playground, Isla." You're loud enough another parent blanches and pulls their child away. That'll teach them not to throw things.

Sighing, you remind yourself to stop thinking like that. Remember the parenting class. "If you want someone to stop, say 'Stop it, I don't like it' and hold up your hand like this." You show her, palm facing away from your body.

"Stop, don't like it," she says in your head, with a sign as big as a roadworker's. Your amusement trickles through in hints of yellow-green and she beams, so you have to take her away from the ball pit before anyone else sees your disciplinary failure.

Kristen is still fixated on my non-love-life. "Does he go bowling? Maybe we should do a double-date sometime."

You don't think so. Sean, her mane-haired boy, drove his father away with his banshee routine before he turned one-year-old. You have a suspicion he's a factor in Kristen's string of bad dates, too. Not that she's the only mum whose child's quirk doomed their parents' relationship. Your own ability has sent every man packing. Well, until Barry. Though you're not quite sure where you stand, there. Or swim.

You smile, collect Isla's puppy-decorated bag, and offer cold chips to Sean to finish off. "I don't know," you say. Kristen's expression is blank and quiet. "He's good at surfing though"—probably; the dolphin skills are likely to transfer to human, you think—"so maybe that could be something."

It doesn't mean anything and you're already regretting the comment, but Kristen's mouth curves tightly nonetheless. She traces Patterns in spilled table salt. "You know, sometimes I think you don't like me very much, Nessie."

"What? Of course I do!" Where did that come from? You shake your head, partly to dislodge the unquiet thought that maybe she heard you. No, you're more careful these days. And anyway, it's not true.

You grab Isla's hand and her backpack, but hesitate before leaving, to try to turn things around. "I didn't mean . . . There's adaptive surfing for wheelchair users, isn't there?" Your chest is tight. "Anyway, single mums need to stick together."

You force a smile. No one else knows about the loneliness. No else seems to care. It was a year ago now, and she's the only one from Parent's Group you can still stand to see. The competition wore you down.

"Yeah." Kristen sounds unsure.

Isla is sending images of donuts and lamingtons into your brain; she's tugging at your hand. *"Stop that,"* you send.

You should stay, make her feel better. Kristen's been on the low since her cat was found dead at the side of the road. But you're running out of words—or thoughts—of comfort. And it's not like anyone's ever given *you* any to show how it's done.

Isla's transitioned to Pop Tops and cheesies now. "Next week, same time?" you ask, already moving away, hustled by your child.

"Yeah, alright, Nessie," Kristen says. Waves.

It's weeks before you realise neither one of you has texted.

* * *

Djeran, again. Season of adulthood. Of change.

You're in a slump. Isla is teething, which keeps you up all night. Your girlfriends are too busy to go out, suspiciously so.

241

It's after Easter and the father of your child is behind on his support payments like he is every damn year at this time. Work is slow. The dishwasher just broke. It's only Tuesday.

When Barry rocks up at six p.m., you almost cry. He brings red wine and salmon, and nuggets for Isla. She shows him her sore tooth; he says the right things and laughs at her telepathic jokes that you can't hear; he sings her old lullabies.

When she's asleep at last, you relax together on the couch with the TV on to cover the sound of kissing.

"What made you come over tonight?" you ask, when lips are swollen and in need of moisture. The wine is half gone. Barry doesn't drink.

He reaches out and strokes your hair. It's not styled today, but he admires it like the brown tresses belong to some fancy actress. He kisses it. "You didn't like dinner?"

"That's not what I—" You pause at the tease in his eyes. "I did. I liked it a lot." This is what he does, now. He comes and goes, with the tide, with the moon. Sometimes it's for weeks, sometimes mere hours. He rarely texts. No Tech wizard has been able to modify or waterproof a phone for a marine mammal's use.

There's a question in his eyes, but you clamp down your walls. He doesn't want to hear your woes. "Let's see if we can find something *you* like," you whisper. Knowing what you're doing, neither minding. You lead each other to the bedroom.

You take it slow. Let him see your bitten nails, your undyed hair, your caesarean scar. He shows you the nub on his back that turns into a dorsal fin. You both laugh.

Love and the quiet night swallow time.

Afterward, he answers your question. "I felt you out there, Nessie."

"Hmm?" You are laying in the crook of his arm, tracing waves on his bare chest.

"You've made a connection. Here." He places your hand over his heart. "I knew you were sad today. Angry. So I came in."

You sit up. "But—"

"Your control is less than you think it is, baby. And I am an Empath, too."

You frown. Your cheeks heat, your fingers grow chilled. Tears form in the corner of your eyes.

"It's not a bad thing," he says, capturing your hands in his.

"But that's so *far*," you whisper.

He smiles. "We both have water in our veins. And you've always been a broadcaster."

"No. I don't know what you mean about water, but I don't Transmit as much anymore," you protest. "I used to. But not now." Not since Isla's father walked away. He'd said he couldn't stand listening to you for one more second. You've worked so hard to smother your voice since then.

"I'm sorry, Nessie," Barry says. He leans up to kiss you, but you pull away. There is hurt in the pool of his eyes.

The room is too cold now, the night too dark. You jump out of bed, turn on the light and reach for a robe.

"You've been able to hear me . . . since we met?" you ask. Oh God, all the little things that have crossed your mind, the tiny spites. The things you thought you'd kept to yourself. He nods, and another chill streaks along your spine. "Have other people, too?" Your panic rises. You can't stop shaking. One glance at his face and you can see the truth.

He gets up. Tries to hold you. "Shh, Nessie, it's alright," Barry says, but your ears are ringing and the words slide straight through. "From what I've learned about Transmitters— and yes, I've done some research, and no, it's not out of concern—from what I've learned, bonds across distance are rare. Maybe it's the Aqua link, magnifying your quirk, maybe something else. And yes, you're a broadcaster, but Nessie, look at me"—he tilts your head—"Baby. You make sales at the kiosk because you love your job and people can *feel* that. Your friends know what you're thinking and continue to be your friends because they like you. Your bond with your daughter is so bright I can almost *see* it."

His hands squeeze gently. "You love and *are* loved, Nessie."

You shake your head. The salt tears are flowing and it's appropriate, really, that you end up drowning because of him.

You think you understand now, why everyone leaves in the end. You never knew.

No one ever said.

The peculiar looks, the falling away of conversation . . . You've been kidding yourself for so long that you'd made it better. No one except *him* ever said a word—and those he did were never kind, nor free from manipulation. Which prompts another thought: *Isla.* The one person to whom you've always Transmitted on purpose, whose bond with you is so strong . . .

Your tears turn to wracking sobs. "My baby," you cry, and Barry tells you to hush or she'll wake, and you cry more.

"Mummy?" Your tiny human stands in the doorway, fluffy unicorn in one hand, rubbing her eyes with the other. Barry hides his nakedness while you run to her, fall on your knees and pull her in tight.

"I'm sorry, *I'm sorry*," you whisper, over and over.

Isla's heard your every thought for two and a half years, her entire life. Every uncensored criticism, every nasty comment, every internal debate. Fury; sorrow; self-hate and spiralling depression. She's probably heard your inappropriate thoughts about a certain dolphin man. Did she hear you the times you wished she'd never been born? When you wished that *you* hadn't?

People are awful, in the deep places inside themselves. No child should be exposed to this side of humanity. You cry for

245

her innocence and your mistake, your blind belief that everything would be okay if you only *kept it in*. You cry because you've been feeling sorry for yourself for so long that you forgot to consider how she felt. You took her bond for granted.

The bond between you is grey and purple and twisted like a hurricane.

Isla squirms away and runs to Barry, who's clothed and silent now in your maelstrom of emotion. "She says, 'Stop it, I don't like it,'" he tells you quietly.

You take a breath, a deep one, but you're suffocating under an ocean of drowning waves. If you close your eyes, can you forget it all? You're an awful mother. A terrible person.

"No, Nessie. You're not a bad mother. You're just you, and you've been doing the best you can." Words. Just words. "She's an Empath, Nessie. She'd have heard it anyway."

Oh, God. You didn't believe it when Barry first told you, but Isla's father's quirk wasn't Empathy, so how could hers be? It had to be *his* secondary. And if so . . . Chalk it up to another thing the bastard hid from you.

Oh, God. Isla never stood a chance.

Fear returns, a tidal wave.

But they are there: the dolphin man and the rainbow child. One holds you up, brings you to the surface. One lights the way with her love the colour of the rising sun.

Morning comes.

The tears dry up. Cold is replaced with the warmth of four arms.

You breathe. It's only the first step in the long swim back to shore. But you are still alive.

You can still fix things.

You can still change.

The alarm sounds, a gentle song to wake the day, and Isla asks for breakfast, hoping for strawberries. Promising all the strawberries she can eat, you hold them close, these people bonded to you. Your daughter, who had no choice, and your lover, who did.

* * *

Djilba (first spring): the season of conception. Wet days and clear, cold nights mixed with pleasant, warm days. Wildflowers grow.

You were wrong, of course. Isla has a choice. Same as how you chose to break away from your mother, and she from you, the choice remains to you both to reverse that decision. And despite your unique Mother-Daughter link with Isla, despite the love between you—or because of it—your daughter will always be able to walk away if she wants to. Her telepathic quirks are both gift and curse, but so are all powers. One just has to learn how to use them.

247

That's the difference between you: a mother who never learned to control her emotion, and a daughter who will be taught everything she needs. Because she deserves it.

But so do you.

You walked past the baby boutique store again yesterday, when Isla was at daycare. She's been going twice a week, enough for you both to practise some distance, some independence. The shop assistant eyed you as you entered. Were you there for a friend, or yourself? For fripperies or expensive clothes or beautiful children's books? Her eyebrows rose when you told her what you wanted. She gave you the number of her old teacher.

You start classes next week on 'How to recognise other peoples' needs'.

It was your father's side that had the Aqua quirk, buried and half-forgotten. And of course, your mother never said. Your doctor had looked at you like a crazy person, thirty-two and asking what your secondary quirk might be, but they'd prescribed the test. Results were clear, as was the advice: stay away from large water sources, unless you want your primary quirk amplified. Ironic, considering where you live. "*Thank you*," you'd Transmitted—to the nurse's distaste—and walked away.

Barry gave you some contacts who might shed more light on this new quirk, and you think you might talk to them. In time.

He left three months ago, hunting offshore for the season. Your dolphin man said he'd come back, but you won't blame him if he doesn't. You've come to understand that it's okay either way. He helped you see yourself, and late as it was, difficult as it was, that was the most important gift you've ever received. If Barry returns, you've vowed to take him bowling. To cook fresh crab from the market, spend a week away with Isla in Margaret River. Watch the ocean and the sunset and just be happy.

And if he doesn't come back? You'll do it anyway.

You bury your face in your scarf. It's rainbow-coloured and made of the softest yarn, almost too warm to wear. Infused with Isla's scent; a simple charm. It's your first successful knitting project. The plan is to make a blue one next, with a gentle wave lapping the edges in green. A matching beanie for Isla for next winter.

Today, your daughter holds your hand as you stroll together along the esplanade. A pelican lands nearby, graceful in the water yet so huge. Its yellow eyes watch you. You wave. Isla hops onto the wall, balancing with exaggerated care as you walk together. Another child floats past in the air, turns a cartwheel over the river, and giggles. Isla laughs too, and you turn to see someone you vaguely recognise hurrying your way.

But no, it's not that woman from Parent's Group last year. She grabs her child, and with a leap she is airborne too, and they are Flying towards a group of friends sitting beneath the foreshore trees. Moreton Bay figs. Imported from the East Coast. Out of place, yet now they belong. You watch, and you hope that someday you can be part of something like that again.

"Mummy, cuddle?"

You turn. Isla has come back and waits with arms outstretched. Golden orange love fills the air between you, sparkling with the winter sun and the joy you have for each other.

Her first words spoken aloud. They aren't a request to receive, but to give.

About the Author:

Emma Louise Gill is a British-Australian speculative fiction writer and coffee addict, living on Gnaala Karla Booja. Her short stories appear in AntipodeanSF, Crow & Cross Keys, Curiouser Magazine, Etherea Magazine, and others. She blogs at emmalouisegill.com and procrastinates on Twitter @emmagillwriter.

Lake Tikitapu - on New Zealand's North Island - is said to be home to a mischievous taniwha, known to devour lone travellers in one gulp.

AT THE AGE OF TWELVE

Casey Campbell

At the age of twelve Jamie visited New Zealand with her family. It was the holiday of a lifetime. She had heard of a freshwater lake which was so blue and clean you could see clear to the bottom on a sunny day, almost thirty meters of fresh water holding nothing more than eels and trout which grew to epic proportions but were impossible to catch. An enthusiastic, young Bulgarian waitress told Jamie of a young princess who dropped her greenstone necklace in the lake. The greenstone was said to rise from the depths, searching for a new princess. Jamie knew she would make an amazing princess.

Jamie demanded to go to the lake so her family stayed in a tiny cabin and endured days of driving rain, New Zealand summers unlike Jamie's Kentucky ones. Her baby sister, Meredith hated the cold water so stayed bundled up with their mother. Jamie didn't mind, it was less worrying about Meredith and more time to focus on her search.

Their accommodation was a simple wooden cabin in a tidy, sprawling campground, only a road away from the lake where a

pontoon covered in fake grass swayed in the wake of the
endless ski boats. The sun finally came out and for two days
Jamie walked the perimeter of the lake and perfected her
swimming and diving techniques, eyes wide in the clean, frigid
water, searching, searching for the magical necklace which
would make her a princess. Then a storm blew in and her
parents could endure no more. It was time to move on. Before
they could leave, Jamie escaped, slipping into her still wet
bathers, the pink ones with a ruffle around the neckline, the
one that made her feel like a princess.

Her father soon found her, and stood on the bleak beach,
the rain lashing the green forest with streams that reached
endless fingers out toward the water. He called for her to
return but Jamie focused on the cold which was seeping deep
into her bones, invading her core and taking what it wanted.
Standing on the pontoon for a final time she turned toward her
father who was motioning for her to come back, his hair
clinging to his balding head. She loved him but craved the
necklace more, would give up all her twelve years for a chance
to become a princess.

A swelling in the water caught her eye. Were there other
creatures in this water? The young Bulgarian waitress had
whispered of the Taniwha that had once resided in each lake,
twenty-foot monsters who feasted on those who entered their
territory. They had scales and hair and webbed feet tipped with
shiny talons that could slice a man in two. Jamie was scared

until the young Bulgarian waitress had laughed and said it was all made up. As likely as the Loch Ness monster in Scotland.

Movement rocked the pontoon then tilted it unnaturally and Jamie fell, sliding into the water, hauled down by unseen hands or caught in an underwater rip which towed her further, deeper into the lake, a watery no man's land.

Kicking and fighting for breath, Jamie was pressed, face down on the slimy lake floor, held against it as if someone was willing her to see. She opened her eyes when her scrabbling grasp found something smooth and hard. Then she was released, popping to the surface like a bubble in a mud pool.

Gasping, she heard her father yelling and realised she was face down on the pontoon, not in the water at all. Dazed and confused, uncertain of what had happened, Jamie pushed to her hands and knees, finding a carved greenstone in her palm. It was thicker than her hand, dry with a fine string of meticulously woven flax turning it into a pendant. She slid it around her neck and returned to the water and the beach, unable to process what had happened.

Her father reprimanded, not noticing the necklace hidden in the pink ruffles of her bathing suit.

She became ill later that day and spent the night in a small-town hospital.

During the night Jamie died and no one noticed. She was twelve and had come so close to becoming a princess. But the princess of legend had stepped forward and forced Jamie from her own body. Jamie little more than a memory left behind in a crystal-clear lake.

* * *

Anahera awoke with a jolt. She was in a white, claustrophobic room. The place stank, a smell that clutched at the back of her throat. Like duck fat left in the sun too long, it cloyed and sickened.

Her father and leader of their iwi, Tutanekai had slapped his fat lips together whenever she complained about rotting food, rubbing his wide stomach and booming about being hungry. Anahera had never liked ripe food, preferred what she could collect herself.

This place was loud, the echoing sounds clubbing her around the ears and making her jolt. She opened her eyes and gazed around in confusion. Where was the lake? Had she escaped? She had been stuck beneath the water for a long time and wanted to be free, no longer a princess or the reason her terrifying Taniwha would rear from the water in search of her, determined to exact his revenge against her father.

She wondered where the greenstone was. The necklace had contained her essence for all these long years and she loathed it as much as the lake and its tainted waters.

Sitting up, she took in the relieved pale faces around her. They were jabbering in some absurd language that was beyond her comprehension. These strangers looked welcoming enough but the eye watering odours and hectic lights, as bright as the sun, made Anahera wonder if she had made another wish to a false god. The last one had promised true love then had bought her a Taniwha, a beast for her beauty. Tuhirangi was no rangatira's son, he was not of heaven as his name suggested, he was reinga, straight from hell.

This environment was overwhelming after the rib crushing water and the drone of the boats that churned the lake in mindless circles, leaving Anahera wishing them ill until the winter chill and silence left too much solitude. Anahera had not been born to loneliness, she was highborn and beautiful, everyone said so, her cold indifference solidifying her rank, and making her a prize desired by all others.

Atawhai, a neighbouring rangatira had negotiated on behalf of his firstborn son, Tuhirangi, when Anahera came of age. Together, prince and princess would unite the families, one day ruling a huge tract of fertile land and all four lakes. They would merge their power and control the biggest iwi the area had ever seen.

Anahera had never met Tuhirangi, no one had, but she daydreamed of her future husband, imagined how handsome he was, what a powerful man he would become, and how her power would grow along with his.

When Atawhai, his wife Ataahua and their entire iwi had arrived to confirm the union, they had bought with them not a human bridegroom, but a Taniwha. The beast remained at Atawhai's back, the rangatira puffed with pride,.

Without warning, Atawhai was slain by Anahera's father, Tutanekai, and with a roar, the Taniwha had fled to the lake, the visiting iwi escaping into the forest. Anahera had been terrified but excited too, knowing her father would keep her safe. Confused, she wondered why her betrothed had not arrived with his father, what had become of Tuhirangi. The meeting was meant to introduce the two and Anahera had spent long weeks pining. Instead, she had been greeted—no, insulted—by the iwi's evil pet.

Later, after food was cooked and the remnants put away, Anahera crept into a meeting, stunned to hear the elderly kaimatua discussing how the Taniwha was Atawhai's firstborn in his true form, his god form. She was speechless. That creature was Tuhirangi? Who Anahera was to be joined with? Tutanekai was outraged that he had not been warned by his own kaumatua. Slaying a water god was desecration. How was Tutanekai to defend his iwi? And grave injustice had been dealt to Atawhai's own family who would be mourning their kaumatua. Atawhai had wanted unification and peace and now he was bones.

Anahera had little interest in the politics and the ramifications from this day. She took to the lake, wondering if the prince in his god form remained near, her romantic heart imagining his man-form. Did he have a man form?

* * *

During the night, Anahera's iwi was slain. Man, woman and child. Anahera was kept as a trophy, a gift to those who had lost their leader.

A foul, early morning wind blew as a young girl found her way to the ponga tree Anahera was lashed to. The child was around six and so skinny Anahera hated these people even more. There was no reason for a child to be hungry in this plentiful land.

"What's your name?" Anahera asked the curious girl.

"Ataahua." She peered at the ground, hands behind her back.

"Are you named after your queen?"

"Something like that."

"You *are* beautiful. Now set me free." Anahera commanded. "We will escape this cursed land and find those who will avenge my people. I will start my own iwi if no one will help, find lost souls or missing spirits to aid me."

Anahera meant every word. She could see the path to her new future and it was bright. She would regain what was lost, recruit those strange bushmen who preferred solitude, and she would destroy every iwi who defied her.

The child, Ataahua spoke, "My son, he is afraid, remaining in the lake. You shamed him and destroyed his father. I convinced him you would accept his true form. Your love and compassion was meant to save us all. Instead you have failed."

"Your son?" Anahera laughed. "You are a child. You are cursed by illness of the mind."

The iwi emerged from the surrounding trees and listened to the young girl's words.

"Not the mind." Ataahua lifted her skinny arms, turning to her people, raising her voice for all hear. "Illness in the earth, our whenua. I am sent in both directions in time to find solutions. Backward and forward, I age and I become younger. Whatever the whenua needs. It asked for peace and instead your people fed it blood."

"We should have been warned," was all Anahera could think to say, her pride all that stopped her from crying with despair. Her purpose now was to keep her people alive in her mind until they could be avenged.

"The earth does not *warn*." Ataahua laughed, her face changing, her nose lengthening as if unable to maintain the façade of a child any longer. "It prepares a story, we korero and we play our parts. Sometimes this makes the whenua happy, sometimes it does not."

Anahera understood then, this wasn't magic, it was insanity. "You want to kill me so get on with it instead of filling my taringa with your nonsense. Eat my bones, take my wairua, my spirit's essence. I am nothing without my people. I will exact their revenge."

This only made Ataahua cover her brown teeth with those dirty hands, amused. Her unblinking eyes not leaving Anahera who flinched at the colour, green like an angry lake. No one trusted green eyes. Anahera's own iwi treating them like portents of coming evil.

"My son will have his revenge first." Ataahua assured her, turning to the iwi before adding, "He will be patient, more than you could ever believe. The earth shall be washed clean and our people will return to power. Then these lands can do as they will. My role is now complete. I will return to the whenua and mourn in peace."

The child, Ataahua, the mother of a Taniwha, turned to leave, the people parting to let her through. Something changed and she spun back, her face now a wrinkled old woman's. "You wanted a warning?" she cried. "New people are coming. They will carve our lands without care for our histories and battles. They will create strange buildings to sleep and eat and shit in. They will scour our land for generations and still my son will await you. Heed my warning but understand your future cannot be changed. You cannot outrun fate or my boy."

"What will it matter to me?" Anahera glared. "I will still be dead, as are my iwi."

Her back now turned, Ataahua said, her voice echoing around the clearing, "My son is lost to me now. Taking to the lakes. Our people will perish in the coming generations, wiped out by battles and accidents. Then the pale people will bring more despair, bugs our eyes can't see and vermin with illness in their blood. *We* will fade but *you* will endure. You are fated to wait until the earth is washed clean of people and your greenstone crumbles to sand. Only then will you redeem yourself in the eyes of my son and be worthy of his trust."

"Your son? What about my iwi? Erased like they mean nothing."

"My son was the way back to the gods!" Ataahua screamed, causing those around her to drop to their knees and avert their gazes. "I curse you," she husked, trying to control her emotions. "You shall wait in the water, tied to your people by your greenstone. Then you have one chance to atone. If you fail then we all fail."

Furious, the prestige of her station giving her more confidence than she deserved, Anahera called, "You will fail too. Your people have destroyed my future and I will never lift a finger to save any of them."

Ataahua chuckled and Anahera got a glimpse of the age-old creature within the skinny child's body. "Wait until you see the white man's world. You will tire of these lakes and crave for my son to guide us all home. You will wish you had accepted him when he came so openly to you."

With the korero ended, Anahera's ankles were lashed to a huge stone with flax. A small waka rowed her to the centre of Lake Tikitapu and she was dropped over the side.

262

AT THE AGE OF TWELVE

Fighting for her life, she hooked her fingers to the boat, screaming when the rowers beat them with paddles. Anahera held herself between two worlds as her fingers were pried away, the stone dragging her down. She held her breath for as long as possible then she let go, falling until the stone settled to the lakebed. Thinking of her iwi she took a moment to say goodbye to this hateful world then inhaled just as a creature swam from the gloom. She cared not for the monster. He would not save her after what had happened between their fathers.

The Taniwha came nose to nose with her. His forked tongue flickered against her lips, and as Anahera fell out of her mortal body she felt the gentle kiss of the Taniwha.

* * *

Anahera awoke with a start. The world around her was undulating, no sound touching her. Debris covered her body and as she sat up rotted flax bindings fell away. She was alive and now she was free. Her arms were weak but she pushed her way toward the sunshine and burst out of the water.

Warm sun touched her face and the Taniwha's iwi loitered near the lake's edge, yet when she reached the shore she could not leave the water, and the strangers would not look at her no matter how much she called to them.

Anahera had no choice but to wait, to despair and to wonder if death would have been better. The Taniwha circled

263

but never came within reach. A threat? A promise? Was he imprisoned too or did he choose to stay?

For long centuries they lived together yet alone, his presence becoming a comfort.

Over time people came, different people with pale skin and strange hair. In winter they hid in their wooden shacks but when the sun shone strong they swum, not noticing Anahera circling beneath them, or the Taniwha watching them from the reeds. They built bigger houses and sat atop boats which plowed the lake, towing people with skin so pale Anahera wondered if they hated the sun.

Sometimes her greenstone floated away on its own. At those times Anahera followed to see where it might take them both. Sometimes people even touched it and Anahera's hope would soar to be free of this cursed lake.

She only needed enough space to kill herself and end this torture. But every time, as if sensing something, the people would pull away before their fingers could close around her carving. She no longer remembered Ataahua's words. No longer cared. She wished only to return to her iwi who were waiting for her, just out of sight.

Then a new girl came, searching, searching for something. Anahera tried to drag her to the depths of the lake, anything to burst her own boredom, but the girl slipped out of her grasp. Then the Taniwha tore the greenstone from Anahera's neck, tossed it to the lakebed and dragged the child to it, pressing it into her palm when she floundered.

Anahera's watery world was ripped apart, the sensation of being dragged from the lake was terrifying. As much as she wanted to end her misery, she had grown accustomed to the monotony. For long moments she was pressed inside the greenstone then with a burst of emotion she was released into the body of the pale girl in the strange clothing.

The child battled to retain control of her body, it was a bitter and long-lasting fight, and in the end, Anahera won because she wanted to live more.

The victory was short lived when Anahera awoke in a strange bed.

* * *

It took months for Anahera to adjust to her new life. The family returned to America, taking Anahera further from her lands than she ever dreamed possible. The flight left her traumatized and needing sedation, pills forced through her pursed lips by the woman who wept and called herself mum. Learning the new language was degrading yet they refused to learn hers, clapping with delight when she spoke basic words like a baby. She disdained them, found each one beneath her but needed time to learn this new world, so it suited her to remain quiet for now, docile and cared for. All the while her fractured soul cried out for Lake Tikitapu. Her Taniwha calling to her when she slept or forgot to concentrate.

Years passed in a blur of consciousness. She had forgotten the aches and pains of being human, the scrapes and hurts. It wore on her yet she endured, knowing this life would at least end, hopeful her soul would go with it and fuck the Taniwha and his hurt pride.

She started school and found it dull, her aggression toward the other children when they would not give her what she wanted an ongoing problem. Doctors were called, people talked about her feelings, but she had never been the same since the strange incident in New Zealand. It was like Jamie had died on that lake and someone else inhabited her body. But brain trauma was like that and what was to be done but get on with life.

Sometimes Anahera studied Jamie's family, feeling no pity. They had lost one insignificant child when she had lost everyone except the Taniwha.

And still he called to her.

So Anahera made plans to be rid of this family who called her Jamie and insisted nothing was her fault. The younger sister was no fool. Meredith avoided her and snapped at her parents when they became overbearing. Anahera learned how to use books and the internet, she asked teachers about the history of New Zealand, her home, fascinated in what had changed since she had been cast to the lake. Remaining focussed she began preparing for the journey home. First she needed her greenstone which these strangers had hidden. When she questioned its whereabouts, she was told it had been tossed away for her own good. It was no use to retain trinkets from traumatic times, reminders of almost losing one held so dear. But she wasn't dear, she was an imposter and she knew they felt it.

Anahera's new body turned eighteen within a blink and she was afforded more freedoms. To claim her new life she needed to reach twenty-one, but time meant nothing, it passed with frenetic speed, willing her home to finish what had begun so long ago.

Trying several jobs was fruitless. Anahera was a princess and refused to be subservient. If the Taniwha could not force her to bow, she would not bend a knee to some fat, greasy girl who examined her chest and asked if she were a virgin.

The boys bored her. No matter how much she derided them they would not quit, as if her indifference was only a challenge to overcome. No one compared to the Taniwha who awaited her return; who would wait until the end of time for something she was still unwilling to give him. If he awaited her love he would wait for all eternity. She loved no one. Her emotions drowned along with her body back there beneath the waka. those paddles still bashing at her fingers.

Anahera was fired from that first job when the girl touched her in the back room. Pressing the girl's forehead to the wall until she cried for release.

"Touch me again and I'll show you the Taniwha in my soul," she whispered, following her to the ground as she collapsed.

It took some convincing but Anahera made her way to university, drinking enough to pass, Jamie's parents paying the bill. A website full of old men paid to watch her take her clothes off, she worked hard and saved hard and was on her way back to New Zealand a week after *Jamie's* twenty-first birthday, the call of the forest, the lake and the Taniwha a constant ache in Anahera's teeth. No matter how accustomed she had grown to this new world she would not miss it.

Not bothering to say goodbye to Jamie's parents or her miserable sister, Anahera climbed aboard the plane with more surety than years before, it still disturbed her that people rode the skies in metal birds but she understood it was safe. Tied around her neck, right at her throat, Anahera's greenstone was where it belonged. It had revealed itself when Meredith had returned from university, drunk and strung out on heartbreak, determined to antagonized Anahera, desperate for a reaction from her emotionless sister. The altercation got physical, yet Anahera had no urge to beat on Meredith. She meant nothing to her, was no part of her iwi.

Years of confusion burst from Meredith in a slurred tirade about how Jamie should have died in that lake, how she had ruined their family, how Jamie had gobbled all the attention leaving nothing for anyone else.

Anahera agreed. Their parents had spent so many years trying to fix their damaged daughter they had neglected the true one they had left.

Bored of Meredith, Anahera had punched her in the long-pointed nose. She had never become accustomed to the thin length compared to her iwi's wide ones, and Meredith's had exploded with blood. She bent forward, screaming until the parents came running, blaming Meredith for goading poor Jamie.

Her next sentence put Anahera's scattered existence back on track.

"You know that *thing* isn't Jamie. My sister died in a shitty lake in some far-off country. Give this stranger back her stupid rock trinket and let her go." Meredith was sobbing now, alone on the ground while her parents observed her as if she were the stranger.

Anahera glared at the people who had suffered more than they would ever know, held out a hand and growled, "Give it to me, now."

There was bickering, Anahera refused to join in. She never joined in, letting the anger and disappointment wash over her.

These people knew little of utter destruction. It had taken her such a long time to understand her own loss and, although she regretted the suffering it had caused these people, she was helpless to change it.

Over the years Anahera had searched the house from top to bottom and followed in quiet interest as the father pried up a floorboard and withdrew her greenstone wrapped in newspaper.

Holding it to her lips, Anahera said, "My name is Anahera. My iwi was slaughtered a long time ago and your daughter sacrificed to allow me to return and avenge them. Do not follow me." She turned away before guilt tugged her to turn back to the three white faces. "I thank you for caring for this body. I'm sorry for your loss."

Then she was gone, uncertain if she was going soft with age.

* * *

Less than a week later she stood on the shores of Lake Tikitapu. It was dusk and autumn, few people around as the cool wind whipped at her hair and the lake surface.

Something near the centre of the lake caught her attention. It could have been a felled tree but Anahera knew better, and the wake, just under the water, heading toward her at speed, showed something alive and bigger than any freshwater fish or eel.

She stepped into the water, ignoring the chill, her heart thudding, catching the scent of the surrounding pines, the ugly trees which had replaced her fallen forest of kauri.

The water was at her waist when the huge head arose before her. Not within touching distance but close enough she could note every mark and scar on his big body.

"This will end." She said in her native tongue. The Taniwha shook his head, struggling to shift his jaw to form words.

"This ends when I say it ends," he growled, the dark eyes hard with ongoing hatred.

"Then I cannot stay with you."

His eyes became small with suspicion. "You lie. All your people lie."

"My people are dead. So are yours. There is only you and me. Kill me to appease your wounded pride if you must. Set us both free."

He lunged, snatching Anahera by a wrist with one of his clawed hands. Ignoring the cuts to her wrist, she didn't fight, instead letting herself be towed to the centre of her lake, grateful to be home, to feel her beloved water fill Jamie's lungs as her body was tossed around as if by a dog, shaken, pushed and pulled.

She awoke on a tiny beach which would not be there if the lake were any higher. Beside her lay a man of around twenty.

Anahera wanted to hit him, to strangle him, to press her greenstone right through his black, evil heart. Instead she stood and shed her wet clothes, draping them in a tree to dry.

Turning to the man, she asked, "What now? What was your big plan? You called me back, you got your revenge. My people are gone. You have blamed me for what was done to your father, even though I was just a child. So what now?"

His eyes were flicking between warm and brown to cold and black with a milky sheen. His jaw lengthened as did his teeth. Then he swallowed and his Taniwha retreated. "You must want me," he said, "It was foretold."

"I don't want you," she sighed, stepping back into the water and rinsing her hands. She was aware she was bending over in front of this man, both naked, she didn't care.

"It is not your decision to make," he told her, eyes sliding back to the water.

"Why?"

"Your family must pay."

"My family are all dead. Our time is over, we lost everything, the white man took it."

"I don't care about the white man."

"You don't care about anything." She frowned. "It's time for you to set us both free. Whether you wish to stay here is up to you. But let me go."

Those dark eyes shifted, confused.

272

Anahera asked, "How long since you regained your man form?"

"I am the Taniwha."

"No, you are a man. You can't even remember why this happened, can you? You trapped us here because your mother said you should be offended. She's dead, long gone. It's your life now. What do you want to do with it?"

"I am the Taniwha. It is my purpose."

"No, it is what you are. It is not your purpose." Anahera lifted the greenstone from around her neck and slashed at the man. The sharp edge bit deep into his bicep and he reached out and snatched her hair, pulling her close.

"You are mine."

"I would rather die."

"You are mine," he repeated and Anahera's stopped up emotions broke free. In one move she pulled out of his grasp and slashed out at the Tuhirangi's throat. It split wide yet his face didn't change as he walked from the sand and into the water, the greenstone in his palm, intricate carvings flashing brilliant green that the overcast day could not explain.

His form changed as he strode into the water, the blood colouring his torso. When he was chest deep he turned and pulled his arm back, then let the greenstone fly with one hard throw, the heavy stone sank into Anahera's chest, piercing her heart and pushing her from Jamie's body.

Gasping for breath she no longer needed, Anahera's scream echoed around the lake but no one could hear her. On the beach she found a body collapsed. Unable to turn away, she remained until Jamie's body was found by a dogwalker then collected by men in blue uniforms. What would Jamie's family feel when they were informed of their daughter's final demise. Would it give them closure? Would they turn their attention to their true daughter? Or was the relationship ruined, family links torn apart by guilt and time?

Taking to the lake she drifted for a long time. Her thoughts scattered as a young girl stepped into the frigid water, her one-piece suit bright enough to catch Anahera's attention. A young father rocked a baby, tired and annoyed, not paying attention to his intrepid daughter who looked around the age of twelve.

This time Anahera would make it work. She would find a way to be rid of this curse.

At her back was the Taniwha. She turned to him, the cut at his neck now a thick scar to adorn his battered body. They glared at each other for several long moments before Anahera kicked away, racing for the shore and the girl, their hands touching, the girl grasping the greenstone as it was thrust into her palm. Her grin as she emerged from the lake on a whoop of delight was soon cut off as Anahera flooded her mind.

It took two days before Anahera awoke in the hospital. This girl was a fighter but she was collateral to Anahera who would work harder this time to find her way out of this curse.

* * *

Back in the lake the Taniwha circled his territory, awaiting the time his mother had forewarned, when Anahera would be broken enough to come to him. Only then would he set them both free, after the time of people.

He was patient, his Taniwha form not seeing time as a line but a guide for his future. The outcome was undeniable. His children awaited for Anahera's return, protected beneath the earth. They too were patient. His mother whispered in his mind, reminding him of his purpose. To return their people to the world when it was flushed clean and they would reclaim all that had been lost.

They had nothing but time.

About the Author:

Casey Campbell hails from the mighty Waikato in New Zealand and spends most holidays in the beautiful lakes of Rotorua. She is a librarian, contributor to several short story anthologies and has published seven full length novels. You can mostly find her on Instagram at caseycampbellwrites.

ABOUT DEADSET PRESS

Deadset Press is an independent publisher of incredible speculative fiction. We provide publishing pathways for emerging writers from Australia and New Zealand, and aspire to shine the light on unique and diverse voices.

You can learn more at:

www.deadsetpress.com

ALSO BY DEADSET PRESS

Annual Anthologies

Beginnings: Aussie Speculative Fiction Anthology Vol. 1

Journeys: Aussie Speculative Fiction Anthology Vol. 2

Revolutions: Aussie Speculative Fiction Anthology Vol. 3

Drowned Earth

Prequel: Shards of Silver by Alanah Andrews

The Rise by Sue-Ellen Pashley

Fire Over Troubled Water by Nick Marone

Submerged City by Austin P. Sheehan

Tides of War by Marcus Turner

The Jindabyne Secret by Jo Hart

River of Diamonds by S. M. Isaac

Salvaged by C.A. Clark

Emoto's Promise by Shel Calopa

Charity Anthologies

Stories of Hope

Stories of Survival

The Zodiac Series

www.ingramcontent.com/pod-product-compliance
Lightning Source LLC
Chambersburg PA
CBHW020353120726
47904CB00002B/541